W9-CMG-882

Shlomo's Stories

Shlomo's Stories

Selected Tales

Shlomo Carlebach

with Susan Yael Mesinai

JASON ARONSON INC.
Northvale, New Jersey
Jerusalem

This book was set in 13 pt. Berkeley Oldstyle by Alpha Graphics of Pittsfield, New Hampshire, and printed and bound by Book-mart Press of North Bergen, New Jersey.

10 9 8 7 6 5 4

Library of Congress Cataloging-in-Publication Data

Carlebach, Shlomo.
[Short Stories. Selections]
Shlomo's stories : selected tales / Shlomo Carlebach with Susan Yael Mesinai.
p. cm.
ISBN 1-56821-215-1
1. Hasidim—Legends. 2. Parables, Hasidic. I. Mesinai, Susan Yael. II. Title.
BM532.C3725 1994
296.1'9—dc20

94-7560

Printed in the United States of America on acid-free paper. For information and catalog write to Jason Aronson Inc., 230 Livingston Street, Northvale, New Jersey 07647-1726, or visit our website: www.aronson.com

In loving memory of

MARION BERGSON STEEG
Miriam bat Bert

Life is eternal and love is immortal.
Death is only a horizon,
and the horizon is nothing but
the limit of our sight.

and

LEON ROTHKOPF

Throughout the inhumanity of the Holocaust,
he maintained his humanity, and spread hope,
life, charity, and love
as part of his everyday service
to God and mankind.

From their families.

Contents

Acknowledgments

Special thanks go to the following, without whom this book would not have been possible:

To Arthur Kurzweil and Jean Pease of Jason Aronson, for bringing this spirited phenomenon into a form—and all the other staff who helped so much.

To Tzlotana Steeg Midlo, for her repeatedly generous spirit, perseverance, and enthusiasm in making this project possible and seeing it through to the end; Joel and Nomi Glick, for donating materials and for providing a writing place for the first drafts of the book; Nehama Silver, for conceiving this project; Adina Friedman, for her goodness of spirit in sharing transcripts; Rabbi Sam Intrator, and Freida Jacobowitz, whose knowledge and precision were essential to finalizing this book.

Thanks also to all those in the international *hevrah* of Rabbi Shlomo Carlebach, especially those in Congregation Kehilath Jacob in New York, Moshav Meor Modiin in Israel, and Reb Shlomo's friends in Jerusalem who keep these stories alive in their own spirited fashion.

And, last but not least, deepest thanks to Neilah Carlebach, whose telling of these tales is exemplary; to Neshama and Dari, who swear every day to tell these stories to their children, and to Raz Mesinai and all the children of our *hevrah*, who will carry these stories to the four corners of the world.

LeHaim!

Preface

The stories assembled in this anthology are among the favorite hasidic tales told by Rabbi Shlomo Carlebach since his career as a teacher, musician, composer, and storyteller began in the mid-1950s. Internationally famed as a performer and the father of modern hasidic music, Rabbi Carlebach first emerged as a master in his own right when he established the House of Love and Prayer in San Francisco in 1967. Among the first to draw thousands of young people back to Judaism, he initiated a movement that now extends worldwide. While Rabbi Carlebach is best known for his teachings and his creative talents as a musician/composer, his gift as a storyteller has received acclaim in New Age retreats, storytelling seminars, and concerts throughout the world where Jew and non-Jew alike have been drawn to these stories and to their wisdom.

Those who have celebrated a holiday like Simhat Torah with Rabbi Carlebach at his family synagogue on West 79th Street in New York City—a night when he embellishes the tradition by rounds of stories about our Jewish ancestors—know the atmosphere in which these tales are "given over." The synagogue is packed. Men and women dance with large Torahs, volumes of Talmud in their arms, to Shlomo's melodies, stopping to catch their breath while Shlomo—who never stops—brings the Seven Shepherds to life. Abraham, Moses, Aaron, Joseph, King David—midrashic tales that illuminate the person are gates through which we pass in a celebration of our Torah. The next morning, generations huddle together under the Rabbi's prayer shawl to say the annual blessing for rain.

Around the world, wherever Shlomo appears, crowds numbering many hundreds squeeze into small rooms to listen until all hours of the morning, while Rabbi Carlebach's lustrous voice inspires and transports his listeners into an ancestral world they had believed lost. The magic of these stories is that each listener believes Shlomo is speaking directly to him or her.

Shlomo Carlebach brings these stories to life with a language and style that correspond to the values of the original hasidic masters. He speaks with a "soul jive," using strange but humorous anachronisms, a peasant earthiness, and a marvelous repetition of a few key Yiddish or ritual expressions to generate an immediate at-homeness with religious experience. Last but not least is the amazing simplicity–yet depth–of these tales, which opens hearts and draws the listener into a world that defies intellect. These are stories that have given life to the Jewish quest, that spark of understanding with a mysterious, miraculous, perhaps even zany wisdom. They are tales that belong to the universe, spoken with a Jewish tongue. In putting them into literary form, I have been true to the hearing of them, for herein lies their power and their soul.

Everybody knows that such stories are for children. As the Zanser Rebbe once said, "If you believe them, you're a fool. If you don't believe them, you're wicked." Our stories stretch between these extremes of innocence and evil, welcoming and encompassing all listeners, whether or not they believe.

Each story is a ritual, a healing event weaving together wisdom and action, the finite and infinite, the world of beyond and worlds in between. The story, like a dream, is a vessel that codifies and transmits precious information, the innermost secrets of the heart. The story is the story of the world–the place of hiddenness where God seeks refuge even as He longs for us to know, to listen to Him, to obey His innermost will.

The prerequisite for the story is that it be lived. Rav Nachman says that a deed done with your whole being never stops happening. It goes on, even after we, the doers of the deed, have finished. A story, too, has that eternal momentum. It can be tapped, unveiled, shown to be alive. And if a story is about *zaddikim*, the righteous men of the past, who better can relate such a tale or bring it to life than another *zaddik*? For when the *zaddik* speaks, he has the power to transform the story into a living event.

The story is real in the moment of telling. It is not an intellectual event, but one that strives for joy, the "holy shiver" effect that reaches the soul. "Does the soul dream facts?" Rav Nachman asks us. The story represents another way of knowing. It addresses itself, not to our hunger for information, but to the need to confirm what we already know.

Thus, we can read a story again, or hear the same tale from a new *zaddik* in each generation, the style slightly transformed by the times. Always there is *teshuvah*, a return—some new insight or stirring inspired by listening. For each time we hear, some restlessness in our heart is abated. Our quest is answered.

"Stories have the unbelievable power of taking us back to the beginning," Rabbi Carlebach tells us, "though the story itself has no end." For the soul has its own reality. It knows that "Messiah is yet to come."

The knowledge concealed in our tales is both the deepest and the most obvious. We make no pretense. As Rabbi Moshe Haim Luzzatto wrote in his foreword to *The Path of the Just* centuries ago:

> The writer says: I have written this work not to teach men what they do not know, but to remind them of what they already knew and is very evident to them. For you will find in most of my words only things which most people know and concerning which they entertain no doubts. But to the extent that they are well known and their truths revealed to all, so is forgetfulness in relation to them extremely prevalent. . . . The majority of men . . . devote most of their thought and speculation to the subtleties of wisdom and the profundities of analysis. Few, however, devote thought and study to the perfection of Divine service—to love, fear, communion and all the aspects of saintliness. It is not that they consider this knowledge unessential: if questioned each one will maintain that it is of paramount importance and that one who is not clearly versed in it cannot be deemed truly wise. Their failure to devote more attention to it stems rather from its being so manifest and so obvious to them that they see no need for spending much time upon it.

"Everybody knows," the Rebbe says, as his audience falls asleep, convinced they've heard this story a million times before and know its cause, effect, and the punch line. "Everybody knows, *yadua*," in fact means "hardly anybody knows." The truth is more "*HaMevin, yavin*," or, "He who understands will understand." For those still *awake*, the phrase "Everybody knows" (the equivalent of "Once Upon a Time") is a signal to "Open your hearts, sweetest friends, and listen to the deepest depths." What follows comes from the wellsprings of the unknown, the original root of Oneness.

In Judaism we speak of two *torahs,* or teachings—the *torah shebichtav,* or written portions, and the *torah shebaal peh*, the oral transmission from the most ancient times. The written portion has order: it comes from the world of laws that regulate and work for the perfection of our being. *Torah shebaal peh* is the hidden *torah,* which has been passed by word of mouth to the chosen, from master to student, prophet to disciple, Elijah to Elisha, one great teacher to the next.

To qualify to receive these oral teachings, one must be truly a "master of the mouth." Even though the written teaching is the basis of law, scholarship, and intellect, the oral law is given highest respect by the most knowledgeable. For, as the Viznitzer Rebbe once said when asked why he received a storyteller before a great scholar: "What is the beginning of the Torah? God is telling us stories." Or, as Shlomo Carlebach now says, "God created the world because He needed to tell stories." He needed to have listeners who would hear Him.

Thus, while the oral tales and teachings have less of the structure and permanence of the written Torah, they preserve their own integrity by carefully guarded transmission. The master proves his skill in the way in which he brings a story to life, using the power of the moment, the presence of those who listen, to further the life of the tale. A true *maseh,* or tale, is like a tent in the wilderness, a cloth held down by strong but simple pegs. It is a *sukkah*, a booth for pilgrims, built according to prescribed rules but decorated to suit the imagination—always with one side open to receive visitors from the realm of the miraculous. We forgo the security of house, four walls, fireplace, for a simplicity and openness that bares the heart. Thus we feel the welcoming wind of prophecy, the blessings of Elijah the Prophet.

The task of transmitting these stories from their oral form into the written word is a difficult and subtle one. It demands a vessel, a design in which the story again comes to life, as if the speaker were with us in the room. Our vessel is the storyteller himself. We have chosen to simulate as best possible the experience of listening to Rabbi Carlebach, whose own belief in these tales and their sources empowers them.

Thus, these tales remain stories of one who is in love with the limitations and wonders of our human experience, the little *yidele* in a world of *galut,* or exile, who yearns for his Temple, his God. Shlomo Carlebach, a descendant of a long line of rabbis, and ultimately of King David, received these stories through his family, the many illustrious rabbis he met as a child in Europe, many of whom died in the Holocaust, and the great teachers with whom he studied in America—Rav Aaron Cotler and the Lubavitcher and Bobov Rebbes, storytellers in their own right. Some of these stories have come also through his extensive reading since early childhood, forming a collection that Shlomo accumulated and began to recreate from memory: "I never read a story more than once. After I'd read it, I'd walk away and begin telling it. I say it as I know and understand it, without going back to the book."

Rabbi Carlebach's talent is his ability to bring these stories into the realm of entertainment—which makes them no less holy. Like everyone's dreams, they are filled with angst—constant questions of survival, food, being able to pay the rent, of trying to live in a hostile environment. Often stories of chase, they are highlighted by comic relief, a clown show that thrives on the unexpected, the miraculous, the depths that come from being a Jew. These tales often defy and transform our sense of God, world, even our religion.

The *hutzpah* of the storyteller is matched only by that of his characters. Every story has its own rules, pointing to hidden patterns, other forces that explain our reason for being. From one story to the next, these patterns change, constantly eluding and defying definition, driving home the message that the ground of our being, our only true knowledge of the One, comes through the fixing of our mistakes—whether in thought or in deed.

For as Rav Shlomo is wont to say: "You may try many things in life but you will find that the hardest thing of all is to be a Jew—and to really know that there is Only One God."

Susan Yael Mesinai

The Storytelling *Yid*

efore he passed away, the holy Baal Shem Tov told all his students their purpose in life, the work each one had to do in the world. Some were to teach Torah, others to become hidden *zaddikim*. But Yankele he told to "go around the world telling stories about me."

Yankele wasn't as excited about this honor as you might think. In fact, he had an anxiety attack. "What! You mean I have to run around from city to city like a street musician, begging people to listen to me! I have a wife and children! How long will I be gone from home?"

The Baal Shem Tov's only reply was to assure Yankele, "It will be very clear to you when your work is done."

And so Reb Yankele went from city to city, country to country, telling stories about his rebbe. Eventually, without knowing why or how, he reached Italy. The Italian Jews had little contact with or interest in the holy Baal Shem Tov or hasidic thought, so there were very few people for whom his calling had any meaning. And yet he kept hearing that in Sienna there was an extremely wealthy man who would pay fifty lira for every story told to him about the holy Baal Shem.

Yankele, the specialist in the field, knew thousands of stories about the holy Baal Shem. So he thought to himself: "Maybe *this* is what the Rebbe had in mind, because if I tell the rich man every story I know, I can retire for life."

Yankele hurried to Sienna and presented himself to the wealthy *yid*. "I want you to know, I can tell you every story known about the holy Baal Shem Tov, because I am his appointed storyteller, chosen from among his closest *hasidim*."

The *yid* was pleased. His face shone with delight. "I cannot tell you what this means to me. Stay with me for the first feast of *Shabbes*, and I will invite all the Jews of the city to hear tales about the holy Baal Shem."

Friday night arrived. Yankele felt very at home with the wealthy *yidele* and so was relaxed. But when it came time to tell a story, his mind went completely blank. After months on the road, telling stories wherever he went, he couldn't remember even one first line. Totally embarrassed, he excused himself.

"Please, Sir. Don't think I'm a liar. I really know thousands of stories about the holy Baal Shem. But—for some reason—at this moment I can't think of one."

Fortunately, Yankele's host wasn't angry, but very understanding. "I'm sure you're only exhausted from your journey. Tomorrow you'll have your strength back and can tell us as many stories about your Holy Master as you like."

To make a long story short, the three meals of *Shabbes* passed without Yankele remembering one event of the many miraculous tales he had previously told about the holy Baal Shem. Even the fourth feast of King David passed without a word.

Yankele was profusely apologetic to his host and totally bewildered by this sudden loss of memory. "I don't know what's happened to me!" The merchant thanked him for his efforts nonetheless and gave him several hundred lira for his troubles.

Sunday morning, Yankele set out for a different city, but he wasn't the same man. His confidence and faith in himself as a storyteller were completely broken. How could he ever, for a moment, forget all he had shared with his Holy Master? It wasn't even possible! And yet it had happened.

A few kilometers outside Sienna, he passed a house with the shutters drawn. Suddenly, a story he had never told before came to mind. Quickly jotting it down, Yankele turned his horse around and raced at top speed, back to the *yidele*. When the servants opened the door, without waiting to be announced, Yankele ran up the staircase of the rich man's villa, shouting like a madman: "I remember! I remember a story!"

But when Yankele saw his host's face, he stopped short. The merchant was pale, his eyes swollen and red with tears. It seemed as if he could barely stand up, as if he were pained by some terrible news.

"Sir! Sir! What's the matter! Has someone in your family died? Perhaps I should come back another time."

"No one died, Yankele. I'm glad you've returned. Please, sit with me and tell me your story."

Yankele, very excited, sat on the edge of the nearest chair and started without hesitation: "It's crazy because I don't know the beginning of this story and I don't know the end. I only know the middle and even that's a little vague. But at least I will have given you something in exchange for your kindness to me."

And here's what he told him:

I was once traveling with the holy Baal Shem when he suddenly said: "Turn the horses around. We have to go to the capital city of another region. The bishop there has called a pogrom to kill all the Jews, and we must help them."

I and many of the *hasidim* were frightened. It is very dangerous to go openly into a town where there's going to be a pogrom. But we went. The shutters on every window in the Jewish Quarter were closed, the doors locked. There wasn't a soul on the streets because every Jew knew that if he showed his face, he would be killed on the spot.

Crowds were gathering in the marketplace. A platform had already been raised for the bishop to give his speech, after which, we all knew, the killing and looting would begin. The Baal Shem chose a house directly opposite the stage and knocked on the door, but there was no answer.

The holy Besht then called out: "It's I, Israel, the Baal Shem Tov. Let me in."

Someone finally opened the door a crack, saw the Rebbe, and drew him—and us—into the house.

"Don't you realize you're risking your life to come here? They want to kill us all!"

"Don't worry," the holy Baal Shem assured them. "I didn't come to endanger anyone."

Once inside the house, the Baal Shem Tov opened wide the shutters and stood, directly in front of the window, to see what was going on. The *yidden* in the house couldn't believe the Rebbe's *hutzpah*. Every two seconds, his hosts appealed to him: "Please, close the shutters. The crowds will see and kill us."

"Trust me. Do you really think I would cause such a thing to happen?"

By this time, thousands of *goyim* had begun to fill the square. I and all the *hasidim* were trembling. We could feel the crowd's hostility, and still hundreds more were pouring into the area to join them.

Finally, the bishop arrived in a procession, which moved slowly through the crowd toward the stage. The holy Baal Shem watched him for a moment, then called for me. "Yankele! Go! Tell the bishop I want a word with him!"

The bishop by this time was nearing the steps to the stage.

"Rebbe!" I cried, "That's insane! I'll never make it to the stage alive."

"Trust me," the Rebbe said. And I did.

It was amazing, like the parting of the Red Sea. I walked straight from the door of the house to just in front of the center of the stage. Everybody stepped back to make room for this one lone Jew. As the bishop stepped forward, I said to him: "The holy Baal Shem wants a word with you!"

The bishop got, *mamash*, pale. He looked stricken. "Tell him I will be with him in a few minutes. But right now, all these people are waiting for me to begin my speech."

I ran back to the Baal Shem and reported: "Five minutes."

The Baal Shem said: "Now."

So I went back though the crowd—just like before. The bishop was being introduced. I had to interrupt him. "The holy Baal Shem Tov says: 'Right now!'"

The really unbelievable miracle was that the bishop got up. He said to his hosts and all the people, "I will be right back." And all alone, without his procession, he followed me through the crowd to the house where the Holy Master was waiting.

The holy Baal Shem and the bishop locked themselves in a room. Hours went by. When the bishop walked out, his eyes were red with tears. He was not the same man who had followed me into the house. And when he left, he disappeared without returning to the stage. There was no pogrom.

The next morning, the Baal Shem Tov, I, and the rest of the *hasidim* left the city. That's all I remember. I don't know the rest.

When Yankele finished telling his story, the rich man began to weep uncontrollably. Yankele didn't know what to do.

"Yaakov!" the merchant cried. "Don't you know who I am?"

Yankele studied his face, but didn't recognize him. "It's true, when I first saw you, I thought I had seen you before. But I've traveled in so many cities and countries, it's hard to know where. . . ."

"I'm that bishop!"

"What? But you're Jewish! How could that be?"

"I was born a Jew, but our family was very poor. There was never any room for me. I suffered so much that I took refuge in the Church. I was very bright and gradually rose to the rank of bishop. Like many converts, I was always ashamed of my ancestry. To prove how Christian I had become, I began a campaign to kill the Jews. I would have succeeded, but the holy Baal Shem knew the truth and stopped me before it was too late. He made me do *teshuvah*, to repent.

"I knew from my sin it wouldn't be easy. As I was leaving the holy Baal Shem, I begged him to tell me how I would know if my *teshuvah* has been accepted in heaven.

"The holy Baal Shem thought for a minute, then answered: 'One day, someone will come and tell you this story, exactly as it happened today. Then you will know that your efforts to atone have succeeded in Heaven.'

"When you first came, I recognized you and was hopeful, because you're the only man outside of myself and the holy Baal Shem who knows this story. When you couldn't remember a story the first night, I realized I hadn't repented enough. *Gevalt*! Was I praying Friday night! *Shabbes*! Before and after every meal, praying for you to remember the slightest detail.

"But when you still couldn't recall even one story, I was frightened. It seemed there was no hope that I would be forgiven. That I would have to leave this world without ever fully doing *teshuvah*, repenting.

"After you left, *gevalt*, did I cry! Then, and then only, did God have compassion on me.

"And you remembered this tale."

Everybody Knows

Everybody knows that the holy Reb Shmuel Kamenka was one of the greatest pupils of Reb Herschel Nedvorner who, in turn, was a pupil of the holy Baal Shem. Reb Shmuel was holy, but he had one sickness, one craziness: he gave everything away. Nothing was left in his house to eat or drink, nor was there ever money to buy more. His food and that for all of *Shabbes* was on credit. The rebbe was in such debt that the grocer, the butcher, and all the shopkeepers finally refused to give out any more food until the holy Kamenka paid his bills. Reb Shmuel's wife came home crying.

His *hasidim* heard of their rebbe's predicament and organized an emergency campaign. In one week they were able to collect ten thousand rubles for the holy Rav Kamenka, enough to pay the rebbe's debts and to support him, his family, and his *hevrah* through many months of *Shabbeses*.

At twelve noon, the *hasidim* proudly presented their rebbe with the money. At a quarter past twelve, the rebbe's *shammes*, or assistant, was told the good news. Overjoyed, he came to the rebbe. "Rebbe, please give me the money to pay all your bills. Let's see, we need a hundred rubles to settle accounts with the butcher."

"I'm sorry, but you're ten minutes too late."

"Too late! How is that possible?"

"Two minutes after I received the money, a poor man showed up at the door needing a dowry for his daughter, so I gave him the ten thousand rubles."

If the rebbe's generosity wasn't too much for his *shammes*, it was certainly too much for his *hasidim*. They stormed into the rebbe's presence and told him to his face: "Rebbe! Please! You know we love you, but you're overdoing it. The first *schlepper* who comes along and asks you? All right, give him five rubles; give him five hundred, even a thousand. But don't give him the whole ten thousand!"

The holy Kamenka sighed. "It's crazy! I know it's crazy. But I can't help myself. I must give everything away. Because this is the great teaching I received from my rebbe, the holy Nedvorner, one of the highest pupils of the holy Baal Shem":

I was barely seventeen when I came to him, after having searched months for a rebbe holy enough to take me by the hand and lead me into the palace of wisdom, to teach me the secret of serving God. I felt he was the one.

I didn't have much contact with the rebbe at first. But from the *heilige* Nedvorner's followers, I began to learn what true holiness meant. They shared with me many secrets, especially the importance of saying *tehillim*, psalms.

"Every Friday morning," they said, "wake up early. Immerse yourself in holy water, pure rainwater in the *mikveh*. Then recite the whole Book of Psalms without stopping. If you do so without interruption, without talking to anyone, your soul will be purified enough to receive the holiness of *Shabbes*."

Every Friday I began the Book of Psalms, but something always interfered. I could never finish on time. So, one Friday I woke up especially early. After going to the *mikveh* and saying my morning prayers, I began to recite the Psalms again.

Everybody knows there are one hundred and fifty psalms and that it takes hours to recite them. I had already reached the one hundred and fortieth chapter without stopping when the rebbe's *shammes* came racing into the room and shouted at me:

"Shmuelik! The rebbe's calling you! Come instantly!"

It was a great privilege to be summoned by the rebbe, but I wanted to finish my psalms. So, even as I prayed, I took a scrap of paper and quickly wrote: "*Heilige* Rebbe, Holy Master. I'll come in a few minutes, as soon as I finish my *tehillim.*"

The *shammes* disappeared with the note. Two seconds later, he was back.

"The rebbe says: 'Either you come now or don't bother to come at all!'" What could I do? Obviously if the rebbe, who was so holy, found it necessary to interrupt my psalms, something must have happened. I ran at top speed to the rebbe's room, imagining that the greatest miracle in the world had happened—the Messiah had come, or at least Eliyahu HaNovi, Elijah the Prophet.

At that moment, I was so full of love for my rebbe I would have done anything for him. But when I ran into the rebbe's room, who did I see, stretched out on the floor, crying, and out of control, but Moishele the Drunkard!

Sweetest friends, let me tell you about Moishele. We, the Jewish people, are not famous for our drinking. But in every little city, there's always one who feels called upon to drink for all the Jews. For the sake of Heaven. It has been said that there are those who drink for the Jews of an entire city, and others, with greater capacity, who drink for those of the world. But Moishele was on such a level that he drank for every Jew since the time of our father Abraham.

And Moishele was crying, groveling, *mamash*, before the rebbe.

The rebbe saw me and called me over to him. "Shmuelik," he said. "Moishele is crying because he has no money for *Shabbes*. He's a drunkard and no one will give his wife anything—free or on credit—for their feast. So I want you to walk around town and collect *tzedakah* on his behalf. Only, whatever you do, don't hand the money directly to Moishele! Give it only to his wife."

I was aghast, beside myself. The rebbe couldn't wait seven minutes until I finished reciting my psalms before ordering me to waste my time on this drunkard! What kind of rebbe was this? A man obviously insensitive to my needs. Insensitive wasn't even the word. The man didn't know what I needed. Just when I was on the brink of holiness, he sent his *shammes* to knock me down to the lowest level, where I should spend my Friday afternoon fundraising for a drunkard.

I was furious and filled with resentment. The whole time I spent walking around town collecting for Moishele's feast, I kept asking myself: "Who needs this?" By Friday afternoon, when I'd handed the money to Moishele's wife, I'd already made up my mind that Saturday night, when we could travel again, I'd take off and look for somebody else to fix my soul.

All *Shabbes* I was angry. I didn't look at the rebbe once and he didn't look at me. Right after *Havdalah*, I packed my belongings. I had just closed the door to my room and was standing with my bundle in my arms when the *shammes*, again, came flying down the hall.

"Shmuelik! Where are you going? The rebbe wants to see you!"

I went with him, but only because I was determined to give the rebbe a piece of my mind.

Before I could say a word, the rebbe addressed my complaints.

"Shmuelik, do you really think I don't know what you're feeling? But the truth is: God didn't need you to recite the psalms as much as Moishele the Drunkard needed you to collect for his wife. God has time, but a man as broken as Moishele has no more time.

"Shmuelik, let me give you a teaching I received from the holy Baal Shem. There's a saying of our Fathers: *If you want to serve God, eat bread, drink a little water and lead the life of pain*. What does this mean? That God created us and this world so we should spend our lifetimes suffering? No! Not at all. The holy Baal Shem—who learned this teaching directly from Eliyahu HaNovi—took the words in this passage to mean: If you see someone in pain, give him life! For what is the closest way to God? Giving life."

"And everybody knows," the holy Kamenka told his *hasidim*, "that for me to give away a few rubles to lift someone up is nothing compared to my rebbe's way of giving life! It wasn't just once in a while. He was always this way. The orphan Feigele lived at the mercy of the holy Nedvorner. This child was beautiful, she had the face of heaven, but *nebach*, she was so paralyzed she could barely walk.

The day after Rosh HaShanah, the rebbe secretly called me in and said: "Shmuelik, take these twenty rubles. Get Feigele's measurements without her knowing. Ask the tailor to make her a winter coat out of his finest fabric. When he's finished, bring it home and hide it in my closet until I tell you to bring it to me."

On Yom Kippur, shortly before *Kol Nidre*, we all came to the rebbe to receive his blessing. Not only his *hasidim* were present but the townspeople closest to him and their children. Everyone was crowded around the holy Reb Hershel. Because Feigele was crippled, she was the last to reach his side. By the time she stood before him, her face was covered with tears.

"*Heilige* Rebbe, holy Master," she cried. "You've cured the whole world with your blessings, but I still have such pain. I beg you, make me well again!"

The holy rebbe gave me a sign to fetch the coat. He put it around the child himself, then stepped back and exclaimed: "Feigele, do you know how beautiful you are? . . . Feigele, you are so beautiful . . . if only you could see how beautiful you are."

And the rebbe kept walking around Feigele as

she stood before him in her new coat, round and round, admiring her, repeating for all to hear: ". . . so beautiful. If only, Feigele, you knew how truly beautiful you are."

The rebbe did not stop praising Feigele until her tears subsided and she began to laugh.

"So you see, *hevrah*," the holy Kamenka explained to his *hasidim*, "I cannot help myself. When I see anyone in pain, I must give them everything—I must give them life."

LeHaim! To Life!

oishele the Water Carrier would come once a year to the Seer of Lublin. *Mamash*, he'd save—every last penny—to go see his rebbe around Rosh HaShanah. I don't have to tell you how people treat water carriers—no *kavod*, no honor, as if they're subhuman. But once a year, Moishele would come to the Seer of Lublin and the rebbe would greet him with so much *simhah*, so much joy and love, he would *mamash* hug Moishele. And this outpouring of love from his rebbe kept Moishele and his wife and family going for another whole year.

One day before *erev* Rosh HaShanah, Moishele set out to see his rebbe. He couldn't wait to come into his presence and receive the holy Seer of Lublin's warm greeting. But when he arrived, the *heilige* Seer of Lublin seemed suddenly very bitter. He barked at the humble water carrier:

"Moishele! Go home! I don't want you here!"

"Rebbe . . . I . . . I . . . but I saved everything just to be with you."

"There's nothing I can do! If you really consider me your rebbe, you must trust me! Go home now!"

What can you do? Argue with the Seer of Lublin? Moishele went away heartbroken and began walking back to his village, crying all the way. He just couldn't make any sense out of what the rebbe had said to him. For him this rejection was like the end of the world.

Later that night, Moishele stopped at an inn to rest. Many *hasidim* were there, on their way to Lublin to see the rebbe. They were so filled with *simhah* at the prospect of seeing their rebbe that they were dancing about with great joy. *Gevalt*!

But when Moishele walked into the room and stood there so sadly, they called out: "Moishele, what's causing you all this sorrow?"

"I can't understand it. The rebbe told me to go home."

Everyone suddenly became silent. A mood of gloom seemed to descend on the inn. One of the *hasidim* finally said: "How long can you be sad? Moishele, *LeHaim*! I wish you the best!"

Then another *hasid* stood up on a chair and said: "Moishele, don't be sad! I promise you this year will be the greatest of your life! *LeHaim*!"

And another and another began to cry out: "*LeHaim, LeHaim,*" blessing Moishele at the top of their lungs. Until all the *hasidim* were shouting so strongly, in chorus, "Moishele! *LeHaim*!" that the sadness that had fallen over Moishele completely lifted.

Everyone started dancing, and Moishele harder than anyone else.

"*LeHaim*! *LeHaim*!"

Then it was time for the *hasidim* to go on to Lublin and for Moishele to continue on foot toward his village. The *hasidim* piled onto the wagon. When they saw Moishele taking off in the opposite direction, one of them shouted to him: "Moishele, don't be crazy! You don't have to listen to the rebbe!

"The *Gemora* says: everything the owner of the house tells you to do, you must obey—except when he tells you to leave the house."

So the *hasidim* pulled Moishele onto the wagon. They traveled together for the rest of the night and arrived in Lublin just before dawn.

When he came down off the wagon, Moishele saw the *heilige* Lubliner standing in the doorway, watching him. He was immediately afraid.

But the rebbe called him over and embraced him: "Moishele, I'm so glad you came back. I've been waiting for you."

"Rebbe, what's this all about—sending me home, then wanting me back?"

The Seer of Lublin answered: "When you first walked in the door, I saw that the Angel of Death was following you. I knew you didn't have much time, so I sent you home to say good-bye to your wife and children.

"But when you met the *hasidim* and they began to say '*LeHaim*' to you, each one's blessing drove the Angel of Death another ten miles from your door.

"Moishele, with friends like you have, you could live forever! *LeHaim*!"

The Baal Shem Mistreats a Jew

verybody knows that Israel ben Eliezer, the holy Baal Shem, taught his *hasidim* to be sweet, never to hurt anyone's feelings. God forbid, you should be coarse and insensitive! If so, then you might keep *Shabbes*, wrap fifteen pairs of *tefillin* on your arms and head, but you would never be holy.

One Wednesday the holy Baal Shem Tov announced to ten of his *hasidim*: "Harness the horses and let's start riding! We're going someplace else for *Shabbes*!"

The group left Medzhibozh and drove for many hours. They'd just reached a little village when the holy Baal Shem Tov signaled for them to stop before a fallen-down shack. The roof was in disrepair, the windows were broken, and it was raining in! Snowing in! Blowing! Nonetheless, a cute *yidele*, Mr. Sweetness Himself—but obviously the poorest Jew in the region—came out to greet them.

"Guests! This is the greatest honor in the world! Please come in!"

As the Baal Shem Tov was climbing off the wagon, he turned to his students and whispered: "No matter what happens, don't tell this man that I am the Baal Shem Tov."

They walked toward the house, and the *yidele*, naturally, asked: "You seem to have traveled so far. Where are you from?"

"Medzhibozh."

"From Medzhibozh! Then you must know the holy Baal Shem Tov!" One of the *hasidim* nodded "yes," but before the *yidele* could ask another question, the Baal Shem Tov interrupted them: "Why so much talk? Can't you see we're starving and want something to eat?"

The *hasidim* were really shocked. The man was obviously a good man, but poor. How could their teacher speak so harshly to him?

The *yidele*, without questioning them further, ran ahead into his house. As the Baal Shem and all his *hasidim* entered after him, they heard the *yidele* in the kitchen say to his wife: "Sarale, the highest honor in the world is ours. We have eleven *yidden* here from Medzhibozh and we must offer them some dinner."

"But we have nothing!"

"We have the milk from our cow."

"That milk is for our children. And the little bread we have left from *Shabbes* is for them also."

Moshe, the *yidele*, answered: "I don't care. Our guests come first."

So Moshe and his wife served their guests the bread and milk. The *hasidim* knew that Moshe was taking food away from his children, so they wouldn't eat. But the Baal Shem Tov made himself at home and ate everything in sight. Whatever they left on the table, he ate—stuffing the food into his mouth until there was nothing left.

The *hasidim* couldn't believe their eyes. They felt very bad for the *yidele* and ashamed of their Master.

The next morning, the Baal Shem Tov woke up early and said: "Hey! Where's breakfast?"

Again Moshe and his wife brought the milk and bread intended for their children. The *hasidim* took only a little, at Moshe's insistence, just to be polite. But the Baal Shem Tov finished off the whole meal. And afterward, he said to Moshe: "I'm really hungry. I'll need a decent meal tonight. You got any meat in the house?"

The *yidele* ran to the kitchen. "I have to offer a decent meal to the eleven *yidden*."

His wife was upset. "The only meat we have is the cow. But we can't slaughter the cow, Moshe, to feed eleven strangers. We won't have any more milk for our children."

Moshe replied: "We can and we will! These

people are my guests and I want to treat them right." So he went and slaughtered the cow himself.

And the Baal Shem Tov, before all his *hasidim*, managed to devour the whole cow Thursday night when they sat down to dine. By Friday there was nothing left but the bones.

Then the Baal Shem called in the *yidele*: "Listen, Moshe! I want to give you my menu for *Shabbes*!"

Everybody knows that on *Shabbes* we offer a special, more extravagant feast than during the week. The *hasidim* didn't know what Moshe would do: he had nothing left. They felt terrible for this poor man who was so sweet. Yet no one had the *hutzpah* to ask the Baal Shem Tov why he didn't show more respect for a man who was obviously in great need.

The Baal Shem Tov said to his host: "I need twelve *challahs*, twelve loaves of bread for *Shabbes*, and three kinds of wine. Two fishes, sweet and sour, and soup for every meal. Chicken as a main course, and cake for dessert. And I expect you to have all this bought and prepared by *Shabbes*."

The *yidele* went back into the kitchen and asked his wife: "What am I going to do? We've got to give our guests something special for *Shabbes*!"

"I have no idea," his wife replied. "We've slaughtered the cow already. What do we have left?"

"There's no other way. I'll have to sell the house."

"Are you crazy! We have children. Where are we going to live?"

"We'll deal with that later. Right now, our guests come first."

The *yidele* went into the village and sold his house. He arranged with the local banker that he could remain on the premises until Monday night. Let's face it. How much can you get for a broken-down house worth only its weight in firewood? Just enough for the three meals of *Shabbes.*

This the Baal Shem and his *hasidim* knew. . . . When they sat down to the table for their first meal on Friday night, the *hasidim* would rather have fasted a hundred years than eat food procured at another's expense. But the Baal Shem, *mamash*, started with the soup and kept right on eating. The *hasidim* couldn't take their eyes off him. "This is our Rebbe? Everything he taught us not to do, he's doing!"

Shabbes passed and it was time to go. The *hasidim* wanted to leave immediately. They saw only too well the pain of Moshe's wife, her anxiety for the fate of her family. But the Baal Shem wouldn't leave until absolutely every crumb of the feast was gone. By Sunday night, there was nothing left on the table or in the kitchen. The *hasidim* felt so bad—a man and his family without house or food—that when the holy Baal Shem gave the signal, they raced to the wagon, eager to get away.

The Baal Shem Tov came slowly behind his students, waved farewell, and climbed up onto the wagon seat. The whole time—can you believe—he had not uttered one word of "thank you" to Moshe for his hospitality. All he did, as the wagon pulled away, was to turn around and shout to Moshe: "I want you to know that I am the Baal Shem Tov!"

All the way back to Medzhibozh, the *hasidim* were silent. They felt they could never forgive the Rebbe for that *Shabbes*.

Meanwhile, standing before his house, Moshe began to realize his fate: "Tomorrow I have to move out! I have nowhere to go; there's no food in the house! My family is starving! What am I going to do?"

One thing was for sure. He couldn't go into the kitchen and consult with his wife, because Sarale wasn't speaking to him. So, as he often did when he had a problem, Moshe ran into the forest to hide. He sat down under his favorite tree and began crying to God: "Master of the Universe! I slaughtered the cow and sold the house just to fulfill Your will, but now I have nothing. Please, God, I don't know what to do. Have compassion on my family. Never mind me! My wife and my family need food and shelter!"

That was only the beginning of Moishele's prayer. Perhaps you know that when you pray, your soul expands. Well, Moshe's soul grew wings. The little *yidele* began to think: "If only I were rich. . . . Then I could have as many people for *Shabbes* as wanted or needed to come, without worrying about how I would feed them."

So he said more to God: "Master of the Universe . . . if you would just make me rich, what I wouldn't do for You in honor of *Shabbes*! I'd have hundreds of guests and I'd offer them the finest of feasts."

Then, filled with desperation and doubt as he remembered the troubles that awaited him at home, the *yidele* put in one last appeal. "Please, God, I'm begging you. Spare my family. This has all been my fault. Please, God, show me what to do."

And Moshe started for home On his way, he ran into Ivan, the city drunkard, who greeted him very warmly. "Hey, Moishele! I've been looking all over the village for you! We have to talk. Have you seen how my children abuse me? They treat me like a dog, call me a drunkard and a good-for-nothing! They have no respect.

"The only person in the world who has treated me like a real human being, Moshe, is you! So I've decided to share a secret with you. I may look like a nothing, but I'm a very wealthy man. I have thousands upon thousands of gold pieces buried in this forest, and I want to show you my hiding place. Because if I die, I want you to have them."

At first Moshe didn't believe him, but Ivan took him to a certain stump in the forest and there, hidden in a hollow covered by a rock, was an immense treasure. Ivan showed him the gold. Then, together, the two men walked home, feeling good.

The next day there was a funeral in the town: Ivan the drunkard had died in the night. Moshe the *yidele* became wealthy then and there—a multimillionaire with plenty of guests for *Shabbes.*

A year passed. In Medzhibozh the *hasidim* could never quite look their rebbe in the eye for the way he had treated Moishele. One day, Moshe's wife said to him: "Moshe, the Baal Shem Tov did all this for us in his crazy way and we've never even said "thank you" or shared our good fortune with him. Let's go visit him."

By this time, Moshe owned a beautiful carriage with eight horses. His children were very well dressed. Food they had in abundance; they didn't need milk from an old cow. So they packed some gifts and went to Medzhibozh to see the holy Baal Shem.

When the carriage appeared before the home of the Holy Master, the ten *hasidim* who had accompanied the Baal Shem that *Shabbes* could not believe their eyes. They recognized Moshe immediately and ran over to him with the warmest greetings: "*Shalom Aleichem*! How are you doing?"

"You won't believe it, but in these few months since I saw you, I've become extraordinarily rich!"

"So we see! What happened?"

Moishele told them the unbelievable story of Ivan's bequest.

"This obviously has to do with the way in which the holy Baal Shem was behaving that *Shabbes*! Still, why did he have to be so gruff?"

They all went inside to meet the Master.

"Moishele," the holy Baal Shem greeted him. "Tell me exactly what happened since I left your house."

So Moishele began with the story of Ivan's bequest. He recounted how he'd gone into the forest and prayed before God to make him rich.

Here the holy Baal Shem interrupted him: "You see, Moishele! You were poor, but Heaven had decreed that you should be rich. You had only to ask. But you were too humble to ever think of your own needs.

"So I ate your cow and got you to sell your house in order to force you to cry out for what was rightfully yours. *LeHaim*!"

Saving a Bride and Groom

*Everybody knows that the first sign of a holy Jew is his humility, how much he thinks he is worth. Because this is the acid test. Let's say, between people, I love my wife very much. But if I'm always thinking what unbelievable things I've done for her, then I'm far from really loving her. The same is true in our relationship with God. If I walk around thinking, "Please, God, give me a chance to do a little good," then there's room for a relationship with Him. But if I think in my heart, "*Oy gevalt*! What I did for God today! I hope He's keeping His books straight," then I'm an outsider. I've left no room for the immensity of God.*

n old woman came to holy Reb Motele, Rav Mordechai of Chernobyl, and said: "Please come fast! My husband's dying and he wants to see you!"

"Dying! God forbid, *has veshalom*!" Reb Motele took ten men and went to see the old woman's husband, a little water carrier, a very simple Jew. But when Reb Motele—who was one of the highest men alive at that time—opened the door to the house and looked into the bedroom, he nearly fainted. He had to lean against the door frame for some time before the color came back into his cheeks and he had enough composure to enter.

Reb Motele sat at the *yidele*'s bedside and the water carrier greeted him. "Forgive me for troubling you, Rebbe, by making you come to me, but I must speak to somebody who understands."

And the *yidele* started to cry.

Reb Motele took his hand. "What hurts you so much?"

"I know that I'm going to die, and I've never done a good deed in my life. What will I tell God when I get up to Heaven?"

"I can't believe you didn't do anything good. I'm sure you've done many *mitzvos* of which you're unaware. Think back over your life and tell me whatever comes to mind," the Rebbe counseled him.

"I can't, Rebbe! It's all so dark! I don't remember a thing."

"Then let's begin at the beginning. Tell me what you did when you were very young. . . ."

Most of what the *yidele* recounted was uneventful until he reached age fourteen: "I grew up in the country. My father was a farmer. I myself was very good with horses. Even the wildest ones I could tame. I was so fearless that I would grab a horse running at full speed and bring it to a halt.

"Once I even stopped a wagon team. I was walking across a field near the highway when I saw a bride and groom—happy, laughing—just returning from their wedding. They were so enraptured with each other, they didn't realize the horses were going too fast. They were already out of control, going at breakneck speed down a hill. If they didn't stop soon, the wagon would turn over and they could all be killed.

"So I jumped, without thinking, into the middle

of the road. When the horses saw me, they were shocked. They drew up for a second and I took hold of the reins.

"'Get off the wagon! Jump!' I yelled to the bride and the groom.

"They jumped and I too leapt aside as the horses bolted free. They raced to the bottom of the hill where, as I had feared, the cart turned over and both animals were killed."

Once the *yidele* had remembered this incident, he gathered strength and went on to tell of other positive events in his life. When he had finished, Reb Motele consoled him: "I'm sure your good deeds will speak well for you when you go before the Heavenly Court. In fact, I want you to promise me that this Friday night, after I make *kiddush*, you will return and tell me how you were judged."

The *hasidim* were astonished by Reb Motele's request. The *yidele* gave his word. Then Reb Motele said *Shema Yisrael* and the *yidele*, *nebach*, took off from this world.

Friday night, after *kiddush*, all the *hasidim* gathered together. They knew of the water carrier's promise to Reb Motele and wanted to see what would happen. Reb Motele was sitting at the head of the table. Suddenly, he turned very red in the face. Then he went pale as a sheet. His face turned red and white, white and red, before he broke into a very wide smile.

When he returned to his normal state, Reb Mortele found all his *hasidim* staring at him. No one spoke.

"Before you can understand what happened to the water carrier, you have to know how holy this man was. When I walked into his house, I saw that the *Shechinah*—the Divine Presence—was with him. The radiance that surrounded him, as my father taught me, comes to only one man in a generation. I realized that the *yidele* was the holy of holies, but the *yid* didn't know this about himself. How could he? A man becomes that much less holy when he makes an accounting of his own goodness.

"This is why I wanted to know what happened to him when he went before the Heavenly Court. For even the highest *zaddik* must put everything—good deeds, bad—upon the scale. The *yidele* kept his promise and returned to give me this account:

"'When I went before the Court, the angels came to me and began setting up the scale to weigh my deeds. I was afraid. Before they could even examine the first deed, there was a great tumult. I turned to see the cart with the bride and groom galloping down the hill. They were going too fast, so fast they knocked over the scale.

"'Then the groom called to me. Without thinking or waiting for the horses to slow down, I leapt upon them and rode straight into Heaven.'"

How a Great Light Is Born

Deep down we're always asking the question: when am I supposed to love, to hate? To be arrogant or shy? When am I supposed to speak, to be silent? Rav Nachman says: If I could get to the roots of loving, to own the roots of my soul, then I would know. For while the parts of the body are many, the soul is one.

If I'm on the level of my soul, of complete Oneness, then I know exactly when to love, hate, or be humble, and when to use my holy hutzpah. *All* yiddishkeit, *all service of God, depends on how much holy* hutzpah *you have within you. The holy* zaddikim *reached so high, not because they knew more or their souls were higher, but because they had this quality of holy* hutzpah. *Those who have this* azut d'kedusha *are actually the most humble people in the world. Their arrogance is not based on what they want but on the knowledge, "This is right." Not even, "I think this is right," for they do not draw their strength from their genius or their stupidity. What they know has nothing to do with self.*

Their holiness comes from doing a deed exactly as it must be done at that moment—with the knowledge that this minute will never come again.

Rav Menachem Mendele of Rymanow was one of the highest souls of the past few hundred years. Many stories have been told as to why his father, a simple man, was privileged to have such a holy son. This is one version:

Rav Menachem Mendele's father was a very poor man. But every person, even the poorest, has one day in his life when commercially and spiritually he can become rich. On that day, the gates are open to him and suddenly he knows just what to do.

So, there was an opening. Reb Mendele's father heard that a certain person had gone bankrupt and was selling his house. That one day, he had a chance to buy a palace for ten thousand rubles. So he went around to different people and told them he wanted to buy the house. "If you'll give me ten thousand rubles, I'll pay you back."

And they thought: "Why not? He's an honest man."

With the ten thousand rubles in hand, he went on his way to conclude the deal, an investment that could make him prosperous overnight. But in those days, sadly enough, a landowner had great power over his tenant's life. If you owed somebody money for rent, that person could kill you. As Reb Mendele's father was going toward the palace, he saw a landowner chaining a little boy and girl to either side of his wagon, like two slaves. It was a heartbreaking scene. The nobleman was shouting and the children were crying, obviously terrified of what he would do to them.

The *yidele* interrupted the landowner to ask: "What's going on? What have they done?"

"Their father hasn't paid rent in three years. He owes me ten thousand rubles, so I'm taking his children to sell them as slaves."

Without thinking twice, the *yidele* asked, "May I buy them?"

"Sure, if you have the money. It would save me the trouble of going to the marketplace."

"Here are the ten thousand rubles. Let them go."

After cutting the children free, the *yidele* blessed them and helped them find their way safely home. But then he himself had nowhere to go. What would he tell his wife, not to mention those from whom he'd borrowed the ten thousand rubles?

"Not only am I no richer, but I owe more money

than I will ever see in a lifetime and have no means to pay anyone back."

It was clear to him that now the children's fate, or Siberia, awaited him if he did not repay his loans.

Reb Mendele's father was so desperate that he went into the *beis midrash* and sat down at a table alone to study. The book was open before him, but he was lost in thought when another man entered the sanctuary—a well-to-do man, perhaps a traveler. The gentleman took out a *Gemora*, a Talmud, and sat across from the *yidele* to learn. From time to time, the stranger looked up at him.

Finally, he said to the *yidele*: "I see you can't concentrate on your learning. Have you troubles of some sort?"

"No. It's nothing. Don't worry about it."

"Tell me. Perhaps I can help you."

The *yidele* was downcast; he had to talk to somebody. So he told the whole story. The stranger listened. "You have no problem. I'll give you the ten thousand rubles right now. Just sell me the *mitzvah*, the good deed, of buying two children out of slavery."

"Are you mad? My deed, and you want to buy it for money? I can't do that."

They continued to learn in silence. But the *yidele* was still distressed. He didn't know what to do.

The rich man suddenly said: "I'll tell you what.

Don't sell me the whole *mitzvah*, just give me half the good deed for ten thousand rubles."

"No, I can't. It's just not right."

"Then, a fourth."

"Please, I realize that you want to help me but I cannot accept."

They continued to learn and to bargain. Finally, the stranger closed his book and stood up: "This is your last chance. Just give me one percent. You'll still have ninety-nine percent left for the world to come."

The poor man simply shook his head no.

The well-dressed stranger got up to leave, but stopped when he reached the door. "I want you to know," he said to the poor *yidele*, "you have shown great courage.

"I am Eliyahu HaNovi, Elijah the Prophet, come when all the gates were open to you to test your goodness. When you gave up your chance for fortune to save those children, there was a tornado in heaven. Because whenever something really good happens, Brother Satan comes to knock it down! He claimed that you were a fake. Maybe you did something good for the moment, but you would regret it. You didn't really do anything for God. So I decided to prove it!

"For giving up all hope of worldly riches to save another's children and then not selling your *mitzvah*, you brought such joy to heaven, I bless you with a son who will bring light to the whole world."

A Meeting on the Road

The Zohar HaKadosh, *the book of Jewish mysticism, says something very deep. In your mind you are either happy or sad. But your soul can be both sad and happy at the same time, laugh, cry, sit, dance, sleep, be awake. For the soul is always one.*

There are all kinds of music in the world. The kind of music that makes you cry and laugh at the same time reaches this oneness within you. But if it affects you in only one way, then you know it hasn't reached you very deeply. It's still in your mind, not your soul.

Reb David Leikes, one of the top pupils of the holy Baal Shem, started out on the road to be with his rebbe for Yom Kippur, the holiest day of the year. But the craziest thing happened. Usually it would only take a day to go from the town where Reb David lived to Medzhibozh, but on this journey, everything went wrong. Every two minutes, one of the horses wouldn't go on, or a wheel broke, or the wagon turned over. Reb David didn't know what was happening.

"I've been on the road three days already. It's really stupid! I don't know what's going on here, but I've got to make it."

Finally, he was only two miles away from his destination. He had exactly twenty minutes to make it to Medzhibozh before Yom Kippur. "Thank God! I can make it if I'm really quick!"

He was crying and begging the horses, "Please

don't make any trouble now. Let's go to Medzhibozh before sunset."

Suddenly, he saw nine people running across a field from a little village, waving to him. They met him on the road. Against his better judgment, he stopped for a second.

And they appealed to him: "We are nine Jews, living in a little village here. We need one more person in order to have ten for our *minyan*."

Some of you know, we Jews need ten people in order to say certain prayers together. Do you know why ten is such a special number? Ten is not like two, three, four, five. It is the first number that is plural and yet is still a single number. One, ten, twenty. Ten is a unit, so much and yet one, like our world. It's the first number that reveals the multiple nature of God's oneness in the world. So we need ten to pray together.

These nine people were *mamash* begging Reb David, "Please stay with us for Yom Kippur."

"Are you crazy? I've been driving for three days already to be with my holy master in Medzhibohz. Please don't be angry with me, but what you ask is too much. I can't help you."

Totally disheartened, the nine men stepped back. Reb David called to his horses and galloped away.

When he arrived in Medzhibohz, everybody was standing in line to wish "Good Yom Tov" to the rebbe. But when Reb David's turn came, the holy Baal Shem Tov somehow skipped over him. "Ach, most probably he didn't see me," Reb David thought to himself.

After Yom Kippur, the Baal Shem again wished everyone a good year. When Reb David's turn came, one split second before he had a chance to hold out his hand, the Baal Shem Tov was already shaking hands with somebody else.

By Sukkot, the festival of booths, Reb David knew this was no accident. He was being ignored by the Rebbe. So he went to his Rebbe, crying. "Please! Tell me! What did I do wrong?"

"How many hundreds of years, David, has your soul been waiting for the chance to *daven* Yom Kippur with those nine men? You *only* came into the world to pray with them!"

Gevalt!

Reb Baruch's *Tallit*

verybody knows that the *heilige* Rav Levi Yitzhak of Berdichev and Rav Baruch of Medzhibozh were the very opposites of each other. Reb Baruch was very civilized. When he *davened*, he barely moved. When he sat with his family at the *Shabbes* table, he was so regal he was the king of the world.

But when Rav Levi Yitzhak prayed, he jumped from one end of the room to another. He would dance, turn around, fall to the ground. At his table, one had to be very careful. You never knew what to expect. In the middle of *kiddush*, he could go absolutely wild, take the wine bottle, pour it up, pour it down, throw the cup into the air.

Reb Levi Yitzhak wanted so much to spend a *Shabbes* with Rav Baruch, the Baal Shem Tov's grandson, that he finally invited himself.

Rav Baruch said: "You can come, but you have

to behave my way. Especially at the table, with my family, you must be very proper."

Reb Levi Yitzhak of Berdichev thought about it. "The only way I can behave is if I don't open my mouth. I won't even pray, except to say 'Amen,' because the minute I *daven*, I'm no longer myself."

So he said to Reb Baruch: "When we're making *kiddush*, don't ask me to say a blessing. Let me be absolutely silent, because it's the only way I can control myself."

The two rebbes agreed. Reb Levi Yitzhak came for *Shabbes*. They *davened* and he only answered "Amen." The praying went beautifully. Everybody was sure that by *kiddush*, Reb Levi Yitzhak would start jumping on the table. But, no, Reb Baruch made *kiddush* and Rav Levi Yitzhak only said "Amen."

Everybody knows that it's a *minhag*, a custom on Friday night, to eat sweet fish and sour fish. The deepest question in the world, and a big controversy among the rebbes, was which fish to eat first. Some said sweet fish, because then you have the strength to bear the sour. Others said: "Let's get the sour fish out of the way, so that the end will be sweet."

But both ways are holy.

Rav Baruch was civilized. He had a little *hasid*, like a waiter, bring the fish on a platter and ask each person which he preferred to eat first—sour fish or sweet. So the waiter came, sadly enough, to Reb Levi Yitzhak and asked: "Do you like sweet fish?"

That's all the poor *hasid* had to ask. Rav Levi Yitzhak said: "Do I love sweet fish? I love *HaShem*! I love only God!"

And he took the whole platter of fish and threw it up to the ceiling. And the fish began to drip onto Rav Baruch's *tallit*, because in those days the big rebbes always wore their prayer shawls for the feast on Friday night.

Everyone was aghast. Everyone, that is, except Rav Baruch who, for all his civilized behavior, would never wash his *tallit* after that feast because, he said, the stains were very holy. "These stains are caused by a Jew who really loves God. How can I wash them out?"

After Rav Baruch's death, the *tallit* was passed from one rebbe to another to wear on *Shabbes*, but never washed. During this century it became so precious that the rebbes only wore it for Yom Kippur. The holy Munkatcher Rebbe, the last to possess it, wore it only for *Neilah*, the final prayer of Yom Kippur. He must have foreseen the destruction that would be coming into the world with the Holocaust. For the holy Munkatcher's last will was to be buried in Rav Baruch's *tallit*, covered with the stains caused by one who loved only God.

The Great Fixer

Something has happened to the world. Our thoughts have turned again to caring for the soul. In Kabbalah, as in the hasidic tradition, you cure the body, but you fix the soul. Curing takes time, but fixing–if you know how to do it–is immediate.

"The Great Fixer" is based on the idea that fixing is the way to utmost joy. Sadness has a bit of pagan dust in it. Because if you really believe that God has the power to fix everything in the world and that your soul can be fixed, there would be no reason to be sad. Sorrow comes when something seems impossible to fix, when we have forgotten how little effort it takes. We Jews believe that if there were just one man in the world who truly knew how to fix, the Messiah would come in an instant.

The story is that the King of the World, the King of Sadness, wanted to see if the world was still in good shape—that is, if everybody in his kingdom was sad. For you know, sweetest friends, what makes a sad person happy? To meet someone else who is sad. What a joy! So the King of Sadness walked all over the world and came back to his capital city ecstatic. His kingdom was invincible. The whole world was miserable. He had not met one happy person.

But as he entered the city, the most horrible thing happened to him. There, on the porch of a broken-down house, on a broken chair before a broken table with a plate that had a few scraps of leftovers, sat a man strumming a guitar and singing. And, no question about it, the man was unbelievably happy!

This was the end! A conspiracy! A revolution . . .

because the King knew as well as anyone that it would take only one happy person to destroy his entire kingdom. Clearly, he said to himself, the man must be watched. Not trusting any of his spies for fear that they would be influenced by this clown, the King decided that he personally must attend to this happy man.

So the King (who always wore a disguise when he inspected his kingdom) walked over to the happy man and said: "Hey, friend! I'd say how do you do, but *who* are you?"

"What! You don't know me? I am the Great Fixer! I can fix anything. I walk the streets of the world and I shout at the top of my lungs: 'I AM THE GREAT FIXER! Is anything broken in your home? Bring me your broken hearts, your broken lives! Bring me your broken world. I'll fix it for you in no time. It won't cost you much! Just a few pennies—only enough to buy myself a feast. *Because the* feastele *must be a* feastele!'"

The King was already nervous. Sad people don't feast. They shovel food down their throats, but to taste—really to appreciate what God gives you to eat—only happy people do that! Only for people of faith is the feast truly a *feastele*.

The King knew what he had to do. He went back to his palace and the next day, when the Great Fixer walked down the streets of the world, yelling: "I am the Great Fixer! Bring me . . . ," the people opened their windows and cried out:

"Shhh! Didn't you hear? The King made a new decree! No more fixing!"

Bad scene, right? The Fixer's out of a job. But a man must have his *feastele.* So the Fixer was walking around the streets of the world looking for a way to make a few rubles, when he saw a well-dressed man chopping wood.

He said to the man: "It doesn't befit a rich man to chop wood. Why don't you let me do it?"

The man gladly gave him the ax. "Be my guest!"

The Great Fixer chopped wood all day, got a few pennies, bought something to eat. And, as Rav Nachman says, "The *feastele* was a *feastele.*"

Evening: the Fixer's sitting in his house in utter bliss, singing a new song, when suddenly the King—disguised as a *schlepper*—is back. "Hey, brother!" The King is sly. "What's new? How was your day?"

"Didn't you hear! The King's gone crazy. He has forbidden fixing! Can you imagine?"

"But you're feasting! How did you manage that?"

"I chopped wood for a few pennies and did such a good job that the man told me to come back tomorrow."

"Interesting. Very interesting," said the King and, excusing himself, he hurried back to Court. Needless to say, the next day when the Great Fixer went to chop wood, the rich man ran over to him, overflowing with apologies. "I'm so sorry. I don't know what happened, but there's a new decree, issued only an hour ago. No more chopping wood for somebody else. A strange rule, but what can you do?"

This was a mess, right? But it didn't stop the Fixer. He said to himself, "I'll have to do something else for the sake of the *feastele*!" So he walked through the streets of the world until he found an elegant woman sweeping her porch.

"What's the matter? Why is a beautiful lady like you sweeping her porch in her party dress?"

"My maid ran away."

"Never mind. I'll help you."

"Gladly," she said as she handed him the broom. The Fixer swept the porch, got a few pennies and—as Rav Nachman says—"The *feastele* was a *feastele*!"

That night, the King reappeared again. "Hey, brother!" he said to the Fixer, "I see you have such a nice *feastele*! What's going on?"

The Fixer shook his head. "I don't know about this king! He's crazier than ever! Now he has a new decree. No more chopping wood."

"That's terrible! So what did you do?"

"I swept floors today, and my boss told me to come again tomorrow."

It goes without saying that when the Fixer came to work the next day, he found that the King had issued a decree against sweeping. Then came decrees against washing floors and raking leaves, peeling potatoes and lifting stones, baking bricks and taking out the garbage. He even forbade cleaning out stables and latrines. Whatever service the Fixer found to do, the King took away from him the next day, until the whole kingdom was falling apart.

But the Fixer had faith. He never gave up hope, not for a moment. So he thought: "If you can't fight him, join him." Now the King, as you know by now, was always angry at someone, so the kingdom was always at war. The Fixer decided to join the Army. But soldiers at that time were paid only once every half year. The Fixer, however, had *hutzpah*. When he came to enlist, he set a condition on his contract. "I'll become your soldier, if you'll pay me two pennies every night."

Enlistment was low. The General said: "It's the first time I ever heard of such an arrangement, but why not?"

So the Fixer became a soldier. He was given a fancy uniform and a big sword and told to report to the barracks every morning at a certain time.

Now the Fixer—being a happy man—wasn't the fighting kind. He hadn't any idea what to do with his sword. But he was a good actor. So, the first day during maneuvers, he marched up and down, waving his sword in the air and pretending to be mean. But actually he was very careful not to hurt anybody.

And that night he was happy. He went to the office, collected his two pennies, and made his *feastele*.

This time, when the King dropped by, he could barely conceal the rage in his voice: "Hey! What's going on? What are you doing? Feasting again!"

"Not easy, either! I told you before. The King's gone insane. . . . He's got so many rules, he's made it impossible for his subjects to work. He's even ruining his kingdom. But I fooled him."

"What did you do?"

"I became a soldier. I'm really against war, but it was my only hope. Now I have a job for half a year."

"But how can you eat? You won't get paid for six months!"

"Not me. I arranged a special deal."

The King, furious, stormed into headquarters that night and declared to the Chief of Staff: "Soldiers get paid only twice a year. No exceptions!"

This time the King made it really hard for the Fixer, who wasn't told that he would get no pay until he came that night expecting to get his money. The General refused to give him a cent or even to talk about it. But the Fixer had to have his feast because he knew: as long as there's at least one person in the world who keeps the kingdom alive with joy, one for whom the "*feastele* is really a *feastele*," the Messiah will come.

Leave it to the Great Fixer to fix everything! On his way home, he chanced upon a pawn shop, marched in, and sold his sword. He made enough money to live for a year! But every soldier must have a sword in order to work. Fortunately the Great Fixer was still a fixer. He bought himself some silver paper, folded the paper over a piece of cardboard, and made an imitation sword, which he stuck into his scabbard.

And the next day, he paraded up and down in his uniform, waving his sword in the air and looking mean. But underneath his helmet, he was smiling. For, after all, the *feastele* was still going to be a *feastele*.

Now we're approaching the end of this tale, my friends, so be patient and open your hearts. The King of Sadness is back.

"So, brother! How are things?" he asks the Fixer.

The Fixer is laughing. "The King did it again. He made sure I wouldn't get paid. But this time I really worked everything out. I pawned my sword and now have enough money to live for an entire year."

But the law of the kingdom is, sweetest friends, if a soldier pawns his sword, he gets the death penalty.

"Aha!" the King thought to himself. "No more worries! I've got this joker right where I want him!" The King couldn't sleep all night, thinking how best to destroy the Great Fixer.

The next morning he called in the prison warden: "Who's to be executed today?" For the world always finds somebody to be killed, especially in a world where everyone's miserable.

"We have a criminal in Cell Block E."

"Good! I will personally supervise the execution! I want to appoint the soldier who is to slay this man."

The next day, the King summoned his army. All his soldiers lined up before him, standing still as could be while the King, dressed up in his royal, regal costume, strutted around. Finally, he recognized the Fixer in uniform. The King went straight over to him and said, face to face: "I, the King of the World, appoint you to kill this man with your sword."

Leave it to the Great Fixer not to get upset. "My dear King, allow me to tell you something. I have never killed a person in my life and I have no intention of ever killing one. You'll have to appoint somebody else."

The King started yelling like a beast. "Are you crazy! Are you going to defy your King?" He started to choke on his own words. "If you don't kill this man this instant, I'll kill you right now!"

Friends, only sad people are really afraid of everyone else. If you're filled with joy, you're not afraid of anything. You're a fixer. Nothing can harm you.

So the Great Fixer said to the King, "My dear King, before I kill this man, I must be certain he's guilty!"

"What do you care if he's guilty or not? I'm telling you to kill him."

At this point, the Great Fixer realized once and for all that there was no reasoning with the King.

But the law is the law: you must not kill an innocent man. So the Fixer turned and appealed to everyone present: "Brothers and sisters, you must remember me! I am the Great Fixer! I used to fix all that was broken in your lives; your homes; your hearts. So you must understand that I know magic. I understand the truth.

"And I know one thing. When a man's guilty . . ." (he put his hand on the hilt of his sword) ". . . my sword is a sword that will kill! But when a man's not guilty, then my sword turns into silver paper in my hand."

He unsheathed his sword and thrust it into the condemned man. The crowd then cheered, for the sword had turned into silver paper. The prisoner went home to his family, jubilant. And the Great Fixer went home to his house, as happy as could be. Then he tuned up his guitar and sang a new song.

And, according to Rav Nachman, "That night the *feastele* was really a *feastele*."

The *Lamed-vav* Tailor

It is said that Adam was created on the first Friday morning. He ate the forbidden fruit late that afternoon, yet was not driven out of Paradise until after Shabbes. *This means he had the light of Paradise for thirty-six hours. On Hanukkah, we light thirty-six candles at the time of greatest darkness to bring another light into the world, the light of Gan Eden. In every generation, there must be thirty-six hidden people, each like a candle, to keep the light of Paradise alive in this world.*

The world has reached such brokenness that today, it's no longer enough for us to be good. We must also be able to fix the world. Imagine that there's a fire but that someone nearby refuses to help because, he says, "I'm not a fire fighter." When there's no fire he may say this, but if there is one, he'd better become a fireman quickly. Otherwise, he's a murderer.

By the same token, we must learn how to fix. But, according to our tradition, in order to fix someone's soul, you must first be ordained by one of the thirty six lamed-vav zaddikim.

Where are they to be found? These are not people who have billboards on the highway or advertise in the Yellow Pages. They look very much like everyone else. Some even go out of their way to disguise themselves, making themselves look so humble or frightened that we shun them. We even question their right to exist. When we run across such a person, we must always ask: "Is this the lowliest of the low, or actually one of the hidden zaddikim?"

ince the *lamed-vav zaddikim* are very often poor, there must always be a holy person to take care of them. The Baal Shem Tov was, from the time of his *bar mitzvah* until he revealed himself to the world, the master of the hidden *zaddikim*. After he died, the Maggid of Mezhirech took charge of all *zaddikim*. When he also passed away, the world was no longer on the level to have only one holy leader.

The Maggid's kingdom was divided among his pupils and Reb Leib Sore's was given the job of collecting charity for the *zaddikim*. His duty was to meet all their physical needs. In order to facilitate his fundraising, Reb Leib had *kefitzat haderech*, the ability to cross the world with amazing speed. One day he would be in Paris, the next, in Safed. No one ever knew when he might come to town.

Yet everybody who was on the level knew: Reb

Leib was not raising money for ordinary civilians but only for the hidden *zaddikim*. Thus, whenever possible, they gave him all they could.

One day Reb Leib appeared in the *beis midrash* in Kiev. "I need three hundred rubles in cash." No one questioned his request. Everybody trusted him, but who had three hundred rubles in his pocket? For most people, this was a fortune.

A young man who very often helped Reb Leib stood up. "Rebbe, I have the money, but only because I saved it to invest today in an opportunity that will make me very rich."

"Listen, friend! Give me your three hundred rubles and, I assure you, God will give it back to you three million times."

The young man still hesitated.

"You want something more? Then ask a favor of me!" Reb Leib encouraged him.

"Rebbe, if just once I could see to whom the money is given. If I could meet one of the hidden *zaddikim*. . . . Not where I'm told years later, 'Oh, remember the beggar who approached you that winter's day, that was your *zaddik*,' but to know that I am in his presence!"

"Well said! I'll certainly grant your request when the time is right," Reb Leib promised the young man.

So the rich man gave Reb Leib the three hundred rubles. And, as promised, he became very rich, so much so he didn't know what to do with himself. Money no longer interested him. His thoughts turned toward leading a more spiritual life.

"I have so much money, I don't have to work. My children and my grandchildren will never have to work. Perhaps I should move to the Holy Land and devote myself to my religious studies."

Torn between the desire for an active community life and one of quiet learning in the Holy Land, he decided to wait until Reb Leib Sore's returned to Kiev to ask his opinion.

Several months later, Reb Leib returned, walked into the synagogue, and went straight to the young man. "*Nu*! Are you as rich as I said you would be?"

"I'm unbelievably prosperous. I have everything material a man could want. But now I'm concerned with something else. Tell me, Rebbe, do you think I should move to Jerusalem?"

"I see the time has come to keep the other half of my bargain," Reb Leib replied. "Ask one of the *lamed-vav zaddikim* rather than me. Saturday, after midnight. . . ."

Reb Leib instructed the young philanthropist to go to a certain back street in Kiev. "There, in the last house, you will find a tailor working. Knock on the door and he will let you in. He will tell you, without your asking, whether or not you should move to the Holy Land."

It is awesome to meet a *lamed-vav zaddik*. The Talmud says that the sun only comes up because

God says "Good Morning" to the world. Prophets from time to time have heard God's voice, but the *lamed-vav zaddikim* can always hear Him speaking to Creation. So to speak with one is frightening because you are addressing a man who hears and knows God.

Saturday, after midnight, the young man followed Reb Leib's directions, entered an unknown quarter of the city, and took a narrow street until he came to the last house. Through the window he could see a tailor, alone, stitching, sewing with utmost concentration. Knowing in advance that the man was a hidden *zaddik*, the young man completely lost his nerve. He didn't know what to say. So he ducked into an alley and began ripping his pants in a number of different places.

Then he knocked. "Excuse me, Sir. I know it's very late, but this is my only pair of pants and they need fixing. Could you help me out?"

"Come in! Come in! I'd be very pleased to mend your pants. Just take a seat in the corner and give them to me."

The young man didn't know that when you hand a *lamed-vav zaddik* tailor your pants to fix, you are actually giving him your soul. The young *yidele* huddled in the shadows, watching the tailor thread his needle. The pants were torn into three pieces, with many small shreds. The tailor laid them out on the table and arranged them. Then he lifted one leg of the pants and began sewing.

As the tailor put in the needle, the *yidele* went: "*Oi*!"

Where did the tailor put the needle? Right through the *yidele*'s soul.

"*Oi*! Do I need fixing. God, I thought I knew what Yom Kippur was all about but—*gevalt*—does this hurt!"

Then the tailor put the needle in from another side. "*Oi vey*! This pain is excruciating! How will I live?"

But when the two sides were back together again, he sighed with relief: "Thank God! I feel so much better!"

And each time the tailor, with adept hands, sewed the pieces together, the *yidele* felt that much more whole.

Suddenly, there was a knock and a young man of seventeen appeared in the doorway. He was dressed like a Jewish prince, in a *cullot*, a golden robe with black velvet trim.

While the *yidele* didn't know the young man, nor was he introduced, the prince was Reb Motele Chernobyl, who was in training to become the next caretaker for the *lamed-vav zaddikim*.

As he worked, the tailor turned to Reb Motele and said: "So, did you learn how to fix?"

"No, not yet." And so Reb Motele kept watching the tailor sew.

This time, the tailor began to mend the whole world. If the *yidele* hurt so much simply from the fixing of his soul, can you imagine how much it hurt Reb Motele to take part in the fixing of the world? Every time the tailor put the needle into his cloth, Reb Motele would say "*Oiiiiii!*" He would, *mamash*, cry. But each time the tailor pulled the seams together, Reb Motele would say: "Thank God! It's over! How can anyone endure the pain of being so shattered, so torn apart?"

Finally the pants were fixed and the tailor held them up for the young man to try on. They fit.

"Tell me," the tailor asked Reb Motele. "Did you learn enough that, next time, you can fix everything yourself?"

"I believe so!"

Then the tailor turned to the rich *yidele*: "Now that your pants are fixed, you can dance in them on the streets of Yerushalayim!"

The *yidele* moved to Jerusalem. Maybe thirty years later, he got very sick. Doctors said he was incurable. He heard of the great *zaddik*, Reb Motele of Chernobyl, and decided to go back to his birthplace to ask the great rabbi to heal him.

He came to Chernobyl and went to Reb Motele's home on Friday night. When Reb Motele walked into the synagogue, the *yidele* recognized him and fainted. The *zaddik*'s followers revived him.

"Why did you faint?" asked Reb Motele, standing over the *yidele*.

"Rebbe, do you remember me? I was there when you got *smicha* from the holy tailor. I remember how the tailor said to you: 'So, Reb Motele, do you know now how to fix?'"

Reb Motele smiled as he corrected the *yid*: "No, he didn't say '*Reb* Motele. . . .' He just said, 'Motele.'"

A Broken Engagement

A *yidele* came to the holy Lubliner and said: "Rebbe, I've been married for eighteen years and I still don't have any children."

The holy Lubliner saw right away that they'd have to force an answer out of Heaven. "Make an accounting of everything you own—the value of each item down to the feathers of your pillows!" he told the *yidele*.

The *yidele* sat down, made an exact accounting, and announced to the Lubliner: "All I have in the world is worth exactly ten thousand rubles."

"Go home," the Lubliner counseled him, "and if your wife agrees, I want you to sell everything. When you have the ten thousand rubles, come back to me and I'll tell you what to do."

A few weeks later, the *yidele* came back. "Rebbe! I asked my wife if she were willing to be poor in order to have children and her answer was: 'What good are possessions without a child?' So we sold everything as you said. My wife is a maid for the time being in somebody's house. Here's the money. Tell me what to do!"

The Lubliner replied. "Sit down. We must talk seriously. This is a matter of life and death."

The *yidele* sat and the Rebbe reflected for a while. "Before you married your wife, do you remember that you were engaged to someone else?"

"Yes. I was once engaged to Rivkale."

"Do you recall how you broke up with her very abruptly, and then four months later became engaged to your wife?"

"Yes, that's true. It all happened very fast."

"The woman, Rivkale, suffered greatly. You won't be able to have children until you've obtained her forgiveness."

"But Rebbe! That was eighteen years ago! I don't even know where she is! But if you—who can see with clear vision to the ends of the world—could tell me where to find her, I'd go right away to ask her forgiveness."

The Lubliner gave him a sharp look.

"Very well, I'll tell you. Go to the fair in Leipzig. Take your ten thousand rubles and there you will find her."

The fair in Leipzig, Germany, went on for only three months of the year. The *yidele* went to Leipzig and looked for Rivkale everywhere. For three months—day and night—he pounded the streets, searched the face of every woman buying or selling, every booth in the marketplace, but he couldn't find his former fiancée.

I don't know if you know what it is like to look for someone important to you, desperately, continuously. Wherever you are, you think she must be someplace else. No sooner do you take up watch in one cafe then you're off, sure she's in another. He ran up to every woman of her height in Leipzig, certain it was Rivkah, only to be disappointed when a stranger turned around. He was a madman by the time the three months had elapsed and the fair was over.

Exhausted and miserable, the *yidele* walked the streets on the last afternoon of the fair. People were taking up their tents, but he still had not yet found Rivkah. A sudden thunderstorm and very strong rain sent him running for cover. He took shelter under an awning. A very beautiful young woman, also seeking shelter from the rain, came under the canopy. He stepped aside to make a place for her.

The girl looked at him with dark, penetrating eyes. "Why is it that whenever I come close to you, you move away?" she asked him, quite sadly.

"*Gevalt*! Rivkale!"

"Ah! You recognize me after all these years. That's good. But you're married now! Do you have any children?"

The *yidele* fell down to the ground and kissed her shoes. "Rivkale, please. In God's name, forgive me for breaking my betrothal to you. I know I've done you wrong and because of that, I can't have children. But won't you forgive me? It was so long ago . . ."

Rivkale reflected for a moment. "It's true. Eighteen years is a very long time. A lifetime. Yes! I will forgive you, if you'll do something for me in return!"

"Anything!"

"My brother is marrying off his daughter in exactly one week. He still lives in the village in Lithuania where we were both born. He hasn't a single penny for the wedding. Buy yourself the best horse you can find. If need be, exchange it along the way. You must get to him before the wedding At the moment when you hand him seven thousand rubles to dower my niece, I will forgive you."

You know, to ride from Leipzig to Lithuania in those days, a man would have to eat, sleep, and pray in the saddle for a whole week in order to arrive on time. But the *yidele* had no choice.

"I'll do it!"

Rivkale started to walk away, as suddenly as she came. "Wait," the *yidele* cried after her. "It's getting dark and it's raining. Can't I accompany you somewhere?"

Rivkale laughed, a strange little laugh, and

shook her head. "No. Where I go, you can't follow."

The *yidele* had no time to lose. He went out, took the package with whatever money he had left, bought himself the best horse he could find for a thousand rubles, and left Leipzig. Day and night he rode, praying in the saddle that he would get to his village before the wedding.

He was lucky. He arrived in his hometown that morning and found that he still remembered where the brother lived.

The brother, meanwhile, was at his wits' end, trying to get ready for the wedding. The lack of funds to dower his daughter was causing him a nervous breakdown. Suddenly, a man splattered with mud appeared at his door, shouting to him: "Thank Heaven! I made it on time! I've brought you the money you need for the wedding!"

The brother thought that the stranger was playing with his feelings. "Please! I don't have the strength for crazy people today. My house is filthy as it is. All I want to do is clean it up for my daughter, so do me a favor and leave."

"No, really. I came to help you."

"Sure–you and all the other *schleppers* in this town. Have a little compassion. I have enough troubles of my own. I don't have the strength for yours."

"But Rivkale, your sister, sent me to you," the *yidele* shouted. "Why won't you listen to me?"

"Now I know you're crazy! My sister's been dead for eighteen years."

The *yidele* sat down. "That can't be true!"

"Sure it's true. My daughter's named after her! You don't believe me? Go, look for yourself in the cemetery!"

"Nahum! Nahum! Don't you recognize me? I was your sister's fiancé for years."

The brother examined the *yidele*'s face more closely, then certain turned away. "Of course I remember you. After you broke your engagement with my sister, she got very sick. She was so in love with you that she wouldn't eat. The night you married that other woman, she died."

"But that's impossible! I just saw her! I spoke with her!"

"You saw Rivkale? Where?"

"In Leipzig! She told me to bring this money to you!"

The *yidele* told the brother the whole story. How the Lubliner had sent him to Leipzig and, obviously, had brought Rivkale down from the other world to help settle accounts between them. How she'd asked that he dower her niece.

And the *yidele* gave Rivkale's brother the seven thousand rubles. Shortly after he returned to Lublin, he and his wife conceived their first child.

There's a teaching from the Ishbitzer Rebbe in the name of the Seer of Lublin in the name of Elijah the

Prophet that says: When you really want to ask someone for forgiveness with all your heart, you can bring them back from the other world. That is what happened here.

But it works for love as well. If you know with all your heart that your soul mate is in this world, then your great love will bring you together from the far corners of the globe.

This is the miracle of how soul mates meet. I bless us all that *we should find our soul mates. LeHaim!*

The Work of Our Hands

In Pshischa near the *heilige* Yerachmiel, the son of the Yid HaKadosh, lived a tailor who was poor, but extremely talented. Ordinarily, a Jewish tailor couldn't be very successful in Poland, but this one was lucky. A nobleman discovered him and took him into his house as his own private tailor.

Sadly enough, his good fortune caused the tailor to move away from his own people and their religious customs. Slowly, slowly, fixing the pants of a nobleman went to his head. He considered himself such a big shot that he stopped going to *shul* or to the rebbe in Pshischa and began to lead a very different, not-so-kosher life.

The nobleman went to Paris on holiday and returned with an absolutely unbelievable piece of fabric for a new suit. "Tailor, I bought you such fantastic material! You must make me the best suit you've ever made in your life!"

The tailor worked day and night to do justice to the fabric. He created an elegant design, cut the material, and basted and sewed the pieces together himself. The whole time he worked he couldn't help priding himself on the fact that he—unlike other *yidden* in his profession—had become the nobleman's private tailor, with the chance to make a suit out of such exquisite material.

And being a highly qualified tailor, it goes without saying that he made what he considered to be an exceptionally beautiful suit.

But when his patron tried on the new suit, he couldn't climb out of it fast enough.

"What did you do to my wonderful material? This suit is disgusting. It gives me the creeps!"

The nobleman was so angry that he threw the suit—and the tailor—out the window. "You dirty, filthy Jew!" he screamed after him. "When I catch you, I'm going to kill you for ruining my cloth." And he meant it.

Let's face it. When you're a Jew and you have troubles, you know just where to go. Back to the rebbe! Even if you haven't kept kosher, even if you haven't seen him for years. The tailor, *nebach*, picked up the suit from the ground and ran straight to Pshischa, to the *heilige* Reb Yerachmiel.

"Rebbe, please! Save my life! My patron has gone crazy. I designed the best suit I've ever made in my life and he wants to kill me!"

The rebbe held out his hand to examine the suit, stretched it across his lap, and studied it for a moment. As he gave it back to the tailor, he said to him: "Go home. Take the suit apart by opening the seams. Then, sew them together exactly as you did before. When the work is finished, go back to the nobleman and ask him to try it on. I'm sure he'll be very pleased."

The tailor went home and did exactly as he was told. He cut open the seams, pulled out the old threads and–rethreading his needle–sewed the pieces together again. He worked very carefully, making certain every stitch was in place. But he cried the whole time because he knew that if the rebbe's plan failed, the nobleman would run a sword through his heart.

Two days later, the tailor appeared before the nobleman with the completed suit.

"Please, noble Sir. Give me a second chance," he begged his patron. "I've remade the suit and I'm sure you will be very pleased."

Reluctantly, the nobleman tried on the suit and buttoned it up. But when he checked his reflection in the mirror, the nobleman smiled. "Magnificent! What a suit! You really outdid yourself this time!"

And he paid the bewildered tailor twice as much for his labor.

The tailor ran back to the *heilige* Reb Yerachmiel

to thank him for saving his life. And to ask: "Rebbe! If I sewed the suit together exactly the same as before, what did I do so wrong the first time?"

The holy Reb Yerachmiel said to him: "Let me tell you something! When the nobleman took you as his private tailor, you became filled with pride. Instead of thanking God for your good fortune, you saw it all as the work of your hands.

"But such arrogance has a terrible smell. Yours was so strong that when the nobleman first put on his suit, even he was sensitive to it. He couldn't get out of those clothes fast enough.

"But the second time, as you worked, you knew your life was in the balance and you cried over every stitch.

"You see—it wasn't your pride but your tears that made this garment so pleasing to him."

A Bit of Charity

here was a time when the Russian police had a very easy way to make money. They would arrest a *yidele*, a Jew, and then tell his community that if they wanted him released from prison, they'd have to put up the bail, meaning the ransom.

As it happened, there was a police chief in Mezhirech who had been extorting funds from the Russian government. Word reached his boss in St. Petersburg who sent his accountant to check the policeman's books. Now, the policeman had embezzled ten thousand rubles. He knew that if he didn't get that money back in the account in twenty-four hours, he would be arrested. So the Russian policeman decided to apprehend a Jew and get the community to put up the money for his freedom.

There were two orphans in Mezhirech who,

until they met each other, had nobody in the world. They became engaged. As neither had any family, the community banded together to give them a beautiful wedding. The *huppah*, as all Jewish weddings, was to take place at night under the stars.

But that morning, as the groom was on his way to the *mikveh*, the policeman stopped him on the street and arrested him. He told all the elders standing outside the synagogue, "If you want this groom to make his wedding, you'd better put ten thousand rubles on my desk by tonight."

The policeman was so determined not to be talked out of the ransom that he even went so far as to hang a sign on his door: "Any Jew who comes to see me without ten thousand rubles in his hand will be shot."

The community was brokenhearted. Ten thousand rubles was beyond their means. Luckily, the three most important pupils of the Maggid of Mezhirech were there at the time: the Alter Rebbe, who was seventeen and not yet a rebbe; Reb Levi Yitzhak of Berdichev, who was already twenty-seven; and Reb Mendele Vitebsk who was a little older, say thirty-one. The three got together in the synagogue and talked.

"We have to get that young man out of jail! Not only because he's getting married tonight, but he's an orphan. He has no one in the world to redeem him."

In those days, there was a great deal of unity in the ghetto, *Baruch HaShem*. While the rebbes were talking, the community thought to band together and sell whatever they could. Upon making an estimate, however, they discovered that if everybody sold everything—houses, cows, chickens, pillows, forks, spoons, coffee pots, even candlesticks—the most they could collect was five hundred rubles. But if selling wasn't going to raise the money, they didn't know what to do. They obviously needed a benefactor.

Now, there was one wealthy person in Mezhirech named Ze'ev, but he was, without doubt, the biggest miser in the world. Ze'ev, *mamash*, never gave away a penny in his whole life. He even had a sign outside his house. "To all beggars: Anyone who trespasses on my property will get shot." And he would do it. The worst was the manner in which he had become rich. In those days, a Jew couldn't get rich on his own. If you wanted to make a fortune, you had to convert. So Ze'ev, without too much reflection, had changed his faith.

The Alter Rebbe, who had been quietly thinking to himself, turned to Reb Levi Yitzhak of Berdichev and Reb Mendele Vitebsk and said: "The only one who can give us the money is Ze'ev the Miser."

"You're crazy!"

"I don't think so! Everything from Heaven

points to him. Besides, there's nobody else with the resources we need."

"What happens when he shoots?"

"He won't shoot. I'm going to see him right now!"

"If you go, you'd better take us with you for protection."

The Alter Rebbe thought it over. "You can come with me on one condition, that I do all the negotiating. Whatever I suggest, you just smile. Don't so much as open your mouths or you will ruin everything."

Although the Alter was the youngest of the three, he was *mamash* very forceful. The others agreed to his terms, though they didn't believe he would succeed. Only the Alter Rebbe felt confident he could get the money.

The first miracle was that Ze'ev the Miser was so shocked to see a delegation of rabbis at his gate that he didn't shoot. The Alter Rebbe spoke. "Forgive us. We wouldn't have the audacity to ask you for help, but we have no choice. This young boy's wedding is tonight He's an orphan. The police chief arrested him for no reason and will not release him unless we raise ten thousand rubles."

Ze'ev the Miser got tears in his eyes. "This is a most heartbreaking story. Certainly, I will help you!" He went into his office and came back with one penny—one lousy, filthy penny, which he had kept around the office for years, for "an emergency."

Reb Levi Yitzhak of Berdichev and Reb Mendel of Vitebsk, *mamash*, wanted to jump down the Miser's throat. A penny! But the Alter Rebbe gave them a sharp look to remind them of their promise. Then he took Ze'ev's hand.

"Thank you so much. You don't know what you've done for this boy. I bless you that God should give you the strength to do more good deeds like this in your lifetime."

The three men left and walked away in silence, deep in thought.

They had gone about half a block when Ze'ev the Miser sent a servant to call them back. "Please, return. I want to help more."

They hurried back. At the door, Ze'ev the Miser fished in his pocket and handed them another penny.

Reb Levi Yitzhak of Berdichev and Reb Mendele Vitebsk clenched their teeth to keep their mouths shut. But in their souls they were yelling: "What *hutzpah*! You think we have time to fool around with your pennies?" Because they knew the clock was ticking and it would take years, at this rate, to raise the ten thousand rubles. But they kept their promise to the Alter Rebbe and didn't say a word.

Again, the Alter Rebbe shook the miser's hand,

blessed him and said: "Thank you so much. *HaShem* will surely reward you for what you have done for these orphans."

To make a long story short, negotiations with Ze'ev the Miser went on for some time. In each round, he offered them another penny. The Alter Rebbe not only was patient but he responded to every coin Ze'ev the Miser offered him as if it were the most significant gift in the world.

Only now came a breakthrough. Ze'ev the Miser began to give rubles! Instead of one penny at a time, it became five rubles, ten, a hundred, a thousand. At last, he had given them the entire ten thousand rubles.

The three rebbes thanked the miser profusely and ran to the police station to save the boy. Not only was the groom happy, but Ze'ev was a transformed human being. His soul had been completely purified. After having had nothing to do with the Jewish community for so many years, he raced into his bedroom to change for the wedding where, of course, he would be the honored guest.

In the meantime the policeman, alone in his office with ten thousand rubles on his desk, began to think to himself: "Why should I turn over these ten thousand rubles to the government agent in the morning? Why not take off and live like a king someplace else?" Because in Russia, in those days, you could get lost very easily.

But the policeman didn't just disappear. As he

made up his mind how to go about it, he drank one glass of vodka after another until he was drunk. Then he hitched up his horse and wagon and started on his way, heading west to a bridge at the edge of the city.

The wedding was in an open field next to the river on the outskirts of town. Here everyone in the Jewish community was celebrating with utmost joy, not only the marriage of the two orphans, but also the groom's freedom—and Ze'ev's return.

The police chief, drunk out of his mind, was in such a hurry to get away from the town that he began whipping his horses like crazy. He crashed into the bridge with such force that he was thrown from the wagon into the river, where he drowned instantly. At that moment, the bag with the ten thousand rubles—which had been next to him on the seat—flew off the wagon into the wedding party, where Ze'ev the Miser was dancing like mad. It landed right at his feet.

Ordinarily, Ze'ev the Miser would have taken back his ten thousand rubles, but he was so happy that he offered the money to the couple as a wedding present.

Later that night, the Alter Rebbe, Reb Levi Yitzhak of Berdichev, and Reb Mendele Vitebsk met again at the synagogue. The two older rebbes asked the Alter Rebbe: "Holy Brother! What happened with Ze'ev? How did you know what to do?"

"Understand! Spiritually, Ze'ev had the strength to give only one penny, but no one would take it. My accepting that first penny gave him the strength to give yet one more. The more he let go, the more he wanted to give, until finally he became so strong—like Abraham—that he was able to give us the full ten thousand rubles."

The deepest torah *is that, as much as you need strength for physical work, you also need spiritual strength for a* mitzvah. *Every time you do a* mitzvah, *a good deed, the capacity to do others grows more.*

The angels say: "Sometimes a person gets angry at another one for doing so little good, not realizing that—alas—the other one lacks the strength to do more."

It's up to us to welcome their little deeds of charity as a way of opening up the gates for them to give much more.

A Share in the World to Come

aftali, a devoted follower of the *heilige* Premishlaner, was a *schlepper*, a poor man. But he had one treasure, his daughter. She was so beautiful that one of the finest scholars in Naftali's community chose her for his bride. Unfortunately, Naftali had no dowry for her. So he decided to journey to his rebbe to seek his advice. He traveled, walking miles all day, until he reached the holy city of Premishlan.

"Rebbe! Good news!" he said. "My daughter's engaged to the finest scholar in our town. Unfortunately, her fiancé's parents and I are both poor. We barely have enough to eat, much less make it possible for him to sit and learn after their marriage. Do you think you could advance me two thousand rubles for the wedding and to start them out in life? I'm sure somehow I could pay you back."

Now the holy Premishlaner would never say "I." He was so humble that he'd always refer to himself in the third person. And so the holy Premishlaner answered Naftali like this:

"Meir doesn't have any money. All Meir has is one ruble. But he'll give it to you. Use it for the first business offer that comes your way."

Even though the rebbe's gift was a modest one, Naftali was a true Premishlaner *hasid*. He never doubted for a moment that the rebbe's ruble would bring him good luck. With the coin hot in his hand, he began his long hike home. He walked all night and reached his town only at dawn of the next morning, just as the sun was coming up. Weary, but not without hope, he stopped to look at his coin.

As it happened, the richest man in town—a terrible miser—came onto his balcony at that very moment to smoke his morning pipe and enjoy the sunrise. He saw, *nebach*, Naftali standing in the middle of the square, turning his coin this way and that as he admired it. And the craziest thought came into the miser's arrogant mind.

"Hey, Naftali," he shouted. "How would you like to do a little business with me?"

Remembering the rebbe's words, Naftali's ears picked up. "Sure! What did you have in mind?"

"How much can you afford to pay for my share in the World to Come?"

Ordinarily, Naftali would have given the miser nothing. The man was not only a penny pincher who gave no charity, but in all his transactions he was known to be cruel. But, as the holy Premishlaner had said to accept the first business offer to come his way, Naftali held high his single coin. "All I have is this one ruble."

"Fine!" the miser said, congratulating himself on robbing Naftali of his only money. "It's a deal!" And he took the coin.

Thinking this the biggest joke in the the world, the rich man went into synagogue that morning and told the congregation: "You'll never believe what I did this morning! I sold my share in the World to Come to Naftali the Schlepper for just one ruble."

The members of the congregation didn't find this very funny. The miser's insensitivity, *mamash*, took their breath away.

"What!" they yelled at him. "You took Naftali's last ruble for your share in the coming world, when you probably don't even have one! And you call yourself a Jew!"

Within the hour, news of the transaction spread all over town. Everyone, without exception, was disgusted by the deal. As it happened, the rich man's daughter was engaged to the handsome son of another wealthy merchant. His daughter was madly in love with her fiancé. But when the prospective father-in-law heard what the miser had done, he sent a note threatening to cancel the wedding: "If your idea of a good joke is to be so inhumane and cruel, I cannot permit my son to marry your daughter and live in your house."

When the miser's wife heard that the *shidach*, the match, was off because of her husband's crass stupidity, she yelled at him: "You thought you were so smart! Now you've ruined your daughter's chance for a happy life! You'd better go to Naftali and fix things fast!"

"But it was just a joke!"

Naftali, who was exhausted from his journey, was sleeping very deeply when the rich man barged in on him. Throwing the ruble onto Naftali's one and only table, the miser shouted at him: "Here's your coin! I'm taking back my share of the Coming World!"

Even half asleep, Naftali knew that this was no way to do business: "Sorry," he replied. "I'm not giving it back! I bought it from you fair and square."

"Okay! So here's two rubles. You've made some money on the deal!"

"Not two, not three. It's mine. That's the end of it."

Okay! The man was a miser, but he knew what he had to do. He went from three to five, to ten, to fifteen in his bargaining, finally offering Naftali twenty-five rubles to buy back his share. And it wasn't easy for him because the whole time, he couldn't conceive that something as intangible as a piece of the World to Come could be worth even a kopek.

And still Naftali wouldn't consent. "I'm not selling it back to you and that's that!" And he threw the miser out of his house.

The miser, rich as ever, pleased that he hadn't had to forfeit even one cent, went home to his wife. "I cannot deal with that crazy *schlepper*! He's a *meshugena*! I offered him twenty-five rubles and he still turned me down."

To make a long story short, the miser's wife and daughter let him have it. His daughter said, "If you spoil my *shidach*, I'll leave this house and never come back!"

While his wife said, loud and clear: "If you don't go back to Naftali and work this out, I'm going before the *beis din* and getting a divorce! With no difficulty, I might add, because everyone knows now how cruel you can be!"

The miser realized he was in serious trouble, not only with his wife but the whole business community. This time, he asked Naftali outright: "Okay, how much *do* you want?"

Naftali thought about it. "Hard to say! To tell you the truth, it would never have occurred to me to buy your share in the Coming World. First, because I have my own share, and second—if I were to buy anyone else's, it certainly wouldn't have been yours. However, the holy Premishlaner gave me a ruble and told me to accept the first business offer that came my way, which turned out to be yours. Obviously, I cannot undo our deal without consulting the rebbe."

By noon of the same day the two men were on their way to see the holy Premishlaner. Only this time, Naftali rode in an elegant carriage. A journey that previously had taken Naftali almost a day to walk, the rich man and Naftali managed in only a few hours.

In Premishlan, the *heilige* Reb Meir listened as the rich man recounted the whole story, including how frustrating it was to bargain with Naftali.

"The *schlepper* said you were the only one who would know how I can undo this deal and buy back my share of the World to Come."

Reb Meir turned to his faithful *hasid*. "How much did you say you needed for your daughter's dowry?"

"And to give the couple a little start in life? Two thousand rubles," Naftali instantly replied.

"Two thousand rubles," the rebbe said to the rich man. "That's what it will cost you to buy back your share of the Coming World."

The miser had no choice. He counted out the money and gave it to Naftali. When he was finished, Reb Meir said to the bewildered miser, "Only *now* have you begun to earn a share in the World to Come!"

The Three Advices of Levi Yitzhak of Berdichev

One of the *hasidim* of the *heilige* Reb Levi Yitzhak of Berdichev, who was a scholar, owed a fortune to the local nobleman, his landlord. There was no way he could repay his landlord, so he got himself a little position—and it's heartbreaking—living away from his family for nine years to pay the debt. At the end of every year he received one hundred rubles in exchange for teaching the children of the family with whom he stayed.

He saved his money and, at the end of his term—thank God—he had nine hundred rubles in his pocket when he started for home. On his way, he passed by the rebbe. Reb Levi Yitzhak of Berdichev invited him to share in his feast. While they were eating, the *hasid* asked his rebbe if he had any teachings to give him.

"To tell you the truth, I have three pieces of advice for you, but it will cost!"

"Cost, Rebbe? How much?"

"Three hundred rubles—each."

"Rebbe, that's all the money I have in the world."

"Yes, but these are very important advices."

The *hasid* had little time to think. He knew to trust the rebbe and so decided to take at least the first teaching. "I'll give you three hundred rubles for the first."

"Cash—on the table."

The *hasid* put the three hundred rubles on the table. Reb Levi Yitzhak leaned forward and said in a whisper: "Listen, brother. Listen carefully. When people ask you where they should go, tell them to go right!"

"That's it?" Crazy—three years of labor for something as simple as that? But by now, the *hasid* was caught up in the learning. He laid another three hundred on the table, half expecting something more elaborate.

Reb Levi Yitzhak leaned forward and said: "I want you to know, if a man of eighty has a wife of sixteen, he's playing with his life."

Okay. Now he knew Reb Levi Yitzhak to be the holy of holies. He put down the last three hundred.

"Don't believe anything you don't see with your own eyes."

At this point, the *hasid* had nothing in his hand, but he trusted the rebbe so implicitly that he departed with a good heart. He'd gone about a mile when suddenly, at a crossroad, he heard the police–cossacks on horseback. They stopped next to the *hasid* and said: "Thieves stole a fortune from a nobleman and we're hot on their trail. Did you see them? Do you know which way they went?"

At that moment, the *hasid* remembered Reb Levi Yitzhak's advice. "Go right!"

The *hasid* kept walking, but soon he heard the cossacks coming after him. This time, when they stopped, they had the thief bound and draped over a horse. The nobleman said to him: "You, *mamash*, saved my business. This man stole hundreds of thousands of rubles and, because of your advice, I was able to get it all back. I want to thank you for your help. Here's ten thousand rubles."

Okay, the *hasid* had already made ten times the money he gave the rebbe. He kept walking, feeling more than good. That night, he stopped at an inn to rest–as he was now able to pay for the best room in the house. And he noticed, as he checked in, that the innkeeper was a man of eighty and his wife, a young girl of sixteen. Which was a warning, of course, to keep his eyes open.

And so he hid in the hall and saw that, in the middle of the night, the young girl let masked men into the back door of the inn, obviously to kill the old man and take all his money. So, *mamash*, he ran fast–shouting to the old man: "Wake up! These men want to kill you!"

When the thieves heard him shout, many of them ran to save their necks. The *hasid* and the old man were able to ward off the few who remained. Afterward, the *alter yid* said to his guest: "How can I ever thank you for saving my life?"

He offered the young man half of his wealth which, since the old man was very rich, came to another twenty thousand rubles.

And so the *hasid* returned to his city a very rich man. But as he hadn't been there for nine years, no one really recognized him. So he began asking: "How's the wife of the scholar so-and-so?" (meaning himself).

"*Oi*," the people said. "Bad scene. Every night at exactly two o'clock a young man comes to her house. Who knows what they're doing in there! Her husband, you know, is away."

But the rebbe had told the *hasid* not to believe anything until he saw it. So that night, he hid in the bushes near his house, only to find that the gossip was right. At exactly two o'clock, a young man appeared at the door and his wife let him in.

In the morning, the *hasid*, who was now so rich, bought a carriage with four horses and drove up to the house. His wife was overjoyed to see him, but he was rather cold toward her.

"I hear terrible things about you—that you're letting in some young man every night at two in the morning!"

"Yes. And do you know who that is? Our son. When you left, we owed so much money to the landlord that he took away our son as a slave. But every night at two A.M., he comes home to learn Torah until dawn. If you don't believe me, wait until tonight and see for yourself."

That night, the *hasid*'s son came home again. He was, by then, eighteen years old. Thanks to his recent good fortune, the father was so rich he could buy his son back from the nobleman.

As the *hasid* laid out the money—cash on delivery—to the nobleman, he realized something. If he had returned with only his earnings, the nine hundred rubles would not have been enough to pay his debt and free his son. He had needed much more.

Buying the rebbe's advices had made it possible to restore his family and live happily, Jewishly, ever after.

You Can't Pray in a Dry *Tallit*

Everybody knows that Rav Menachem Mendele, the holy Kotzker Rebbe, was so holy he could force you to break through to the deepest depths of your soul. Naturally, if you wanted to be a Kotzker *hasid*, it wasn't enough to go to the *mikveh*. You had to wash out your *kishkes* four times a day. Because the holy Kotzker saw that a sinner who's honest with himself is much higher than a fake holy man.

One of the highest Kotzker *hasidim* was the holy Reb Yechiel Gastenina. Once, when someone asked him how he came to be a Kotzker *hasid*, the Gastenina told this story:

When I was fourteen, I got married. My father-in-law's gifts to me were a *tallit*, a prayer shawl, and a pair of *tefillin* written especially for me. I was so moved by his gifts I swore to myself that whenever I put on my *tallit* or *tefillin*, I would have only the holiest thoughts.

In those days, I used to sit all day in the *beis midrash*. I'd wake up at four o'clock in the morning, go to the synagogue, study a few hours, and then learn, pray, and study again. By two o'clock in the afternoon of each day, I would have studied for eight hours.

Early one afternoon, a *yidele* walked into the *beis midrash*. From the audacity with which he walked, I knew he must be a Kotzk *hasid*. The *yidele* walked straight over to me and said: "Young man, can you loan me your *tallit* and *tefillin*? I haven't prayed yet today."

I thought to myself: "It's two in the afternoon and he hasn't prayed yet! What kind of *hasid* is this?"

So, I told him outright: "I'm only fourteen years old. I've already prayed twice today and studied for eight hours. What were you doing that you haven't even *davened* yet?"

"Brother," he said, "I don't need your advice. Either you give me your *tallit* or you don't."

The fact is that when someone asks to borrow your *tallit*, you have to give it to him. But I was very hesitant, because I'd never loaned it to anyone before.

"My *tallit* is very precious to me. I guard it carefully and have sworn to have only the holiest thoughts when I pray," I warned him.

Oy, did he look at me.

"Then maybe I should ask someone else."

"No! No! Here! I give it to you gladly."

Needless to say, I expected any man who started praying at two in the afternoon to pray like mad. And from what I'd heard of Kotzk, I anticipated an atomic explosion, praying like I'd never seen in my life. But the Kotzker *yidele* put on the *tallit* and *tefillin*, slowly walked over to the large open window, and stared down into the marketplace, idly watching the people below.

I thought to myself: "What a desecration of God's name, to stand by the window and look out at the square. For that he has my *tallit* and *tefillin*! Who knows what kind of thoughts he has running through his head!" It was all I could do not to run over and tear off my *tallit*.

The Kotzker *hasid* stood at the window for at least an hour without praying. Then, very suddenly, he turned and ran up to the holy ark and threw his face into the curtain.

"Finally," I said to myself, "he's really going to *daven*."

The man held his face between the curtains of the holy ark, and in exactly four minutes by the clock, he was finished. That was too much for me. A Kotzker *hasid* spends one hour in my *tallit* staring out the window and four minutes holding his head between the curtains of the *aron*?

I ran over to him and tore off my *tallit*. Both my prayer shawl and the curtain were wet, completely soaked with his tears. *Gevalt*! *Gevalt*! Was I ashamed of myself!

"Please, forgive me!" I cried. "I didn't know you were praying like this! I thought you were only looking out the window!"

"Come!" the man said. "Let me show you something!"

He led me to the window, and together we looked down on the market square where ten cossacks were doing their basic training.

"Watch these ten little cossacks," the *yidele* said to me. "As the officer orders them—left, right, left, right—*nebach*, they go. Young man, do you know what a cossack is? He's a little drunkard and his officer is an even bigger one. If the officer tells him to go right, he would get wounded fifty thousand times before he'd go left. If the general, who's a bigger drunkard than all the cossacks put together, told him to go right, he would get killed in action before he'd go left. And if the czar of Russia told the cossack to go right, he would commit suicide before he'd go left. Isn't it so?"

I nodded my head.

"So I thought to myself as I watched these cossacks: How is it that I stood on Mount Sinai and heard God telling me to go right, but I am still going left? With that thought in my heart, I began to pray."

As the *hasid* finished explaining his prayers to

me, he noticed how I clutched my *tallit* to my heart and that I seemed very upset.

"Don't worry!" he assured me. "Your *tallit* will dry by tomorrow!"

At that moment, I couldn't control myself anymore. I began crying from the depths of my heart. "No! I don't want my *tallit* to be dry ever again!"

The *hasid* put his arms around me and said: "Ah! You really want to *daven*! Then pack up fast and come with me to Kotzk!"

The Wind

verybody knows that the holy Roptchitzer was the right-hand man of the Seer of Lublin. The holy Roptchitzer was very tall, which was helpful when he was ushering people into meetings with the holy Lubliner because he could stretch his arm across the door frame, forcing the visitor to pass underneath. If the person was really humble, the Roptchitzer would keep his hand high so the visitor could enter freely, without any problem. But if the guest was known to be arrogant, the Roptchitzer would lower his arm so the visitor would have to stoop in order to pass.

As for those who, *mamash*, had great delusions about themselves . . . the Roptchitzer would put his hand on their heads and push them down so they were practically crawling on their knees as they came before the holy Seer of Lublin.

The holy Seer of Lublin, in turn, did honor to the spiritual stature of the Roptchitzer by calling him "*heilige* Roptchitzer" even though he was only his assistant, his right-hand man. "Holy Roptchitzer" is how he always referred to him, except one *Shabbes* afternoon when he called him "Ropchic!" And this is the story:

That Friday night, one of the thirty-six hidden holy people, came to the Seer of Lublin and said: "My wife had a baby and tonight is the *shalom zachor* to celebrate his birth. But there is no *minyan* where I live. . . . "

The Seer of Lublin called out: "*Heilige* Roptchitzer! Gather together a *minyan* to go to the home of this little Jew!"

The Roptchitzer, understanding immediately that the *yidele* was a *lamed-vavnik*, chose the eight best pupils of the Seer of Lublin. He went himself, with the *lamed-vavnik*, to make the tenth man for the *minyan*.

The group walked to the outskirts of the city. Halfway to the home of the *yidele*, they were crossing a large field when a terrible storm rose without warning. The wind was so powerful it threw dust into their eyes, making it impossible to move or to see. Most of the group wanted to give up, but the holy Roptchitzer wouldn't let them. Instead, he yelled at the storm. "Wind! What kind of *hutzpah* is this? We're going to the home of a holy hidden Jew for a *shalom zachor* and you're in our way! Take off!"

And the wind ceased.

The next morning, the city was struck by a terrible pestilence that affected the animals. There was an epidemic: the horses and cows were dying. The livelihood of the entire city was affected. Everyone was worried; no one could think of anything else.

When the Roptchitzer came into the synagogue, the Seer of Lublin wouldn't acknowledge him. Whenever the Roptchitzer looked at him, the holy Seer of Lublin would turn his head away. Or, if he needed something from his right-hand man, the Seer of Lublin would say in a very abrupt way: "Hey, Ropchic! Bring me the wine!"

This went on all morning: "Ropchic! Ropchic!" in front of everyone.

The Roptchitzer started feeling smaller than small, but he didn't know what he had done wrong. He had taken the men to the *shalom zachor*, just as his teacher had asked. The evening had been beautiful; they had returned in time for prayers in the morning.

By late afternoon, when his teacher finally called for him alone, the Roptchitzer was desperate. "Rebbe! What have I done?"

"Ropchic!" the *heilige* Lubliner called out as the

Roptchitzer came near. "Do you have any idea how many tears I cried before God to send a wind strong enough to carry the pestilence away, so that no plague would strike Lublin?"

The Roptchitzer was ashamed.

"Ropchic, if you don't know what the wind is for, don't touch it!"

The *Mikveh Yidele*

In the deepest depths, humor is a little bit of the taste of the coming of the Messiah. Because when the Messiah comes, our mouths will be filled with laughter. Everybody knows that the name Yitzhak, Isaac, means in Hebrew "laughter." Isaac was always overflowing with laughter, and yet he was strength upon strength, the sternest character in the world. Yitzhak's world is like the one we will see after the Messiah comes—a world of perfect judgment and absolute laughter.

he Maggid of Mezhirech once told his *hasidim* to hitch up the wagon because they were going far away to Lemberg for the funeral of a *mikveh yidele*. But who cares about a little *yidele* who puts a fire in the *mikveh* stove once in a while or scratches your back when your soul won't reach that far? The holy Maggid recognized his *hasidim*'s reluctance to take part in this *mitzvah*:

"You never know whom you are honoring!" the Maggid reminded his *hasidim*, as their wagon magically traveled a distance of days in only a few hours. "Maybe you should hear more in order to understand better who this man really was."

There once lived near our village a tailor, Moishele, who had an immense amount of charm. He was very adept at fixing the suit of a nobleman, but he really endeared himself by cracking jokes with his customers and getting them to laugh. In short, he had the makings of a really fine entertainer.

One of his patrons liked his jokes so much that he invited him to his castle.

"Moishele, you really are a top-notch comedian. I'm having a big party tonight. You come, tell a few jokes, and I'll give you a salary."

So Moishele said good-bye to his wife, who was very devoted to him and whom he loved very much, and went to the party. He told a few jokes and his act went over in a big way. After the jokes, people began to crowd around him, murmuring something like "*LeHaim*!" A man in uniform pressed a glass of wine into his hand. He knew he shouldn't drink because the wine was certainly not kosher. But this was his first success and, as the crowd assured him, he deserved to be happy and celebrate. So he drank.

Then someone offered him a sandwich.

"What's that?" he asked, pointing to the pale layers of meat peeking from between two slices of rye.

"Ham. What! You never had any before? Then you must try some. It's delicious."

The tailor thought to himself: "Lord, I shouldn't take any, but the *goyim* like me so much. Do I have the right to push the fact that I'm Jewish in their face?" So Moishe ate a little bit of ham and drank more wine—just to be polite—and then returned to his lovely wife and everything was fine.

A few weeks later, another nobleman said to

him: "How would you like to come to my party and be the hit of the evening?" So he went to another castle. This time Moishe's performance was even greater, as he was relaxed and felt more at ease with his audience. His jokes had the guests rolling and stomping in the aisles.

Afterward, of course, he celebrated with a little more wine and a few more sandwiches, just to show his appreciation to his host. And at every party after that, Moishe allowed himself to indulge a bit more, until soon he very often came home drunk.

One night he was standing at a party filled with beautiful women when he had a terrible thought: "Why should I go home tonight? Here are the most gorgeous women in the world. They flirt with me and they love my jokes. All I have at home is my old wife, Hannah. A *yenta*! *Gurnisht*!"

The truth is that Hannah was exceedingly beautiful in her own right and a very holy woman. But Moishe couldn't appreciate her anymore. He had fallen all the way down. He'd given up being a tailor to become a full-time comedian. He'd stopped going home except to change his shirt or pick up another suit. And when Hannah, who cared for him so much, asked why, Moishe felt so guilty he would yell at her.

And when she clung to him, begging him to stay, he'd beat her.

So Moishe, a man of good humor and charm, became wretched and violent—because he had lost his holiness.

One night, Moishe's main patron said to him: "Moishe, sorry to tell you, but your jokes are getting stale. I think it's time you create a new act."

The next day, as it happened, the Baal Shem Tov came to town. Moishe, hearing the news, had the bright idea of imitating a holy man. As the nobility were always expressing their curiosity about someone as charismatic as the holy Master, this showed promise of becoming the act of the year.

So instead of partying, as had become his new custom on Friday night, Moishe left his decadent friends and went to pray with the holy Baal Shem. Actually he didn't go to pray. He went to watch the holy Baal Shem in order to imitate him—to make fun of how he jumped when he danced, how he bowed when he prayed.

But how can you mimic pure joy? Friends, do you know the difference between the laughter of Messiah and that caused by a comedian? A comedian gets on stage and makes jokes about pain, divorce, a man who has lost his shirt. And everyone laughs. But inside they are crying. For his jokes have a taste of death in them. Such laughter is inspired by a comedian who is halfhearted, divided between Good and Evil.

As we say in the Psalms, when *Mashiach* comes, "Our mouths will be filled with laughter." Full, not just from the corners of our mouth.

Everything that came out of the lips of the holy Baal Shem was whole. From the Tree of Life. The tears and the laughter of the holy Baal Shem Tov cut right through Moishe's soul, suddenly making him feel unsure of his art.

"Maybe prayer is too subtle for a quick comic routine. Let's see how a holy man eats at his feast," Moishele thought to himself.

Friday night's feast, the feast of Abraham, was always a time of great joy among the *hasidim*. Moishe tried to push his way into the room, but he was blocked. The *hasidim* knew what he had done to his wife, how he had fallen away from being a Jew. The whole community hated him.

Only by threatening to use his connection with the various noblemen could Moishe get into the room. Once inside, he had the *hutzpah* to elbow past everyone and sit right under the Baal Shem Tov's nose.

Moishe sat there, taking mental notes, trying to capture a few facial expressions, some gesture of the hand during *kiddush* and *motzi*, to design the act of the season—an imitation of the greatest *zaddik* of his time.

Once, the Baal Shem Tov turned very suddenly and stared straight at Moishe as if he knew that the comedian's only reason for being present was to find a way to make fun of him. But then he ignored him and went on with the joys of *Shabbes*.

Finally, the holy Baal Shem Tov began to give a teaching for *Shabbes*. Pretending to be interested, Moishe leaned forward in his chair, adopting a pose of rapt attention. Even as his mind raced with ideas of how to characterize the *zaddik*, Moishe couldn't help being moved by what he was hearing.

Something began to stir in his soul, against his will. Every word from the Baal Shem Tov's lips was so strong, it did something to him. Moishe suddenly saw that there was something much deeper to life than charm or making fun, than being a tailor or a comedian. And he understood how hollow his own life was by comparison.

"Everybody knows," the Baal Shem Tov began to explain, "when you're in your mother's womb, an angel comes with a candle to teach you the Torah that is yours for a lifetime. Unfortunately, when you are born, you forget all you have learned. Only those who find their rebbe will be able to remember, for he will teach it to them again, word for word."

Moishe suddenly understood: Although he had begun to lose his soul, his connection to God, the holy Baal Shem had been speaking directly to him, giving Moishe his instructions from the womb. His life as a comedian became a nightmare.

Instead of realizing his own holiness, what had he become? A wife beater, a drunk, one who mocked the sacred.

Moishele was so filled with remorse that, right after the feast, he ran over to the holy Baal Shem and weeping, begged him: "Please! Help me! Tell me how I can do *teshuvah*!"

"From now on, you must fast from *Shabbes* to *Shabbes*. Stay in the *beis midrash* during the week and only go home on Friday night."

"How long will I have to do this?"

"God will give you a sign."

Right after *Shabbes*, Moishe went to the *beis midrash* and began to fast. Unaccustomed to such adversity, he died a thousand times during the week. By Friday afternoon, he was completely delirious. All he asked of those around him was that they wake him up after the service and take him home to eat.

"But, sadly enough, the congregation forgot him. The *shammes* locked the *beis midrash*. Moishele was lying on the bench, slowly dying. In the middle of the night, he woke up. When he realized that the *beis midrash* was locked and he couldn't get out, he knew he wouldn't last until morning.

Thinking he had only a few more minutes to live, Moishe began praying and doing *teshuvah* like never before. His *teshuvah* was so strong that Elijah the Prophet appeared to him and said: "In a few minutes someone will come to take you home.

After *Shabbes* is over, I want you to move to Lemberg. They need a *mikveh yid*. Don't worry about being alone there, because I will come every night to teach you."

A few minutes later the *shammes* arrived, out of breath and apologizing: "I was fast asleep, Moishele, when there was a knock on my window and someone yelled: 'There's a man dying in the synagogue! You'd better run fast!'"

The *shammes* helped Moishe get home, but Hannah wouldn't let him in. She was afraid he would beat her again. Moishele was at the end. The *shammes* cried: "Can't you see . . . he's dying!" So Hannah agreed to let him stay in the kitchen while she hid in the other room. But when she heard him make *kiddush*, she knew that her old Moishele had come home. The comedian had been greatly transformed.

After *Shabbes*, they moved to Lemberg. Moishe became the *mikveh yid* and Elijah the Prophet came every night to teach him. Now the rabbi in Lemberg was also a great kabbalist. Sometimes, late at night, he would walk through the ghetto. One night, he passed the house of Moishele and, with his holy eyes, saw a heavenly light shining out of of the window. He told his *shammes*: "Go! Find out who lives there!"

The *shammes* walked into the house and said to Moishe: "The rabbi of the city wants to speak with you!"

The rabbi said to Moishele: "I see a heavenly light coming from your house. Is Elijah the Prophet teaching you?"

Out of respect for the rabbi, Moishele told him the truth: "Yes. He comes every night."

The rabbi could not restrain himself: "Moishe—I'm beseeching you—as the rabbi of this city, ask Elijah the Prophet if I may join you. I will be back tomorrow night for an answer."

The next night, Moishe gave the rabbi Eliyahu HaNovi's reply. Although the rabbi wasn't yet on the level to study with him directly, each morning the *mikveh yid* was free to teach him what he had learned from the prophet the night before.

A few days later, the rabbi of Lemberg said to Moishe: "Please tell Elijah the Prophet that I need a sign that these teachings are from the Holy Side. For the Evil Side can also teach Kabbalah."

Elijah the Prophet gave the rabbi a sign, and this is what he said: "As long as I come every night to this city to teach Moishele, no one in this city will die." And for a long time, no one did.

So when the rabbi was called to a funeral, one morning, he knew right away: "*Oy vey*! It could only be Moishele, the *mikveh yid*."

And so the Maggid of Mezhirech took his *hasidim* to console the wife of the holy *mikveh yid*—a *baal teshuvah* who, with the help of the holy Baal Shem, reached a level of holiness in one week that 99 percent of the *yidden* never achieve in a lifetime.

Yankele the Thief

In Medzhibozh there lived a *yidele* known as Yankele Ganef, Yaakov the Thief. Yankele was one of the *hasidim* of the holy Baal Shem. Before the Baal Shem Tov came along, Yankele stole from just about everyone. But after he met his holy master, he began to develop principles and so would only steal from the very rich. His specialty was to steal from traveling noblemen—which wasn't very difficult because Medzhibozh was a favorite stopover on the highway east.

Okay, you steal. But one day, you reach a point where it's not enough to steal one hundred rubles or a thousand. You want to steal something more substantial. Yankele's dream was, just once, to have the privilege of stealing fifty thousand rubles.

You remember, I told you once how a thief was asked on Yom Kippur: "Aren't you the least bit ashamed to stand before God when you've been robbing us blind all year?"

The thief answered: "No, I'm not, because I tell God straight. Master of the World, let's face it. There will always be thefts in this world, so please—since I'm one of the best—let me take care of them."

Yankele was, *mamash*, a dedicated thief in this respect. He never denied his profession before God, and God in turn seemed to watch over him. Every time Yankele Ganef was reckless and got himself into trouble with the law, he'd run to the holy Baal Shem and confess. Once he'd received his master's blessing, the police somehow would forget the whole affair.

It was Shavuot, late spring—the time of the revelation of the Law on Mount Sinai. A fancy nobleman on his way to St. Petersburg passed through Medzhibozh. As Yankele's luck would have it, the nobleman decided to stay overnight at the inn. Yankele immediately organized his *hevrah* of thieves. They took a ladder, climbed to the nobleman's room, and made off with his treasure chest. Yankele broke into the box, only to discover that he had just made off with fifty thousand rubles.

Let's face it! How many thieves were there in the town of Medzhibozh who went around proclaiming their great dream of someday stealing fifty thousand rubles? The police knew immediately who had done the job, and soon they were hot on Yankele's trail.

Was Yankele afraid? Not at all. He took off to

find the holy Baal Shem, thinking that once again his master would shield him and that this would be the end of it. So, the day after Shavuot, he ran into the *beis midrash*. The *hasidim* were sitting around—listless, solemn, silent.

"Hey, everyone! Where's the holy Baal Shem? I have an emergency and need him to bless me fast!"

The *hasidim* just stared at Yankele. Finally one said: "Where have you been? Don't you know the holy Baal Shem Tov passed away yesterday?"

It suddenly became painfully clear to Yaakov how holy the Baal Shem Tov had been. Rav Nachman of Bratslav makes the distinction between a *zaddik tahton*, a low *zaddik*, and a *zaddik elyon*, a high *zaddik*. A low *zaddik* loves only holy people, but a *zaddik elyon* loves everybody because he is, *mamash*, like God.

The Baal Shem Tov was such a *zaddik*. He could love Yankele Ganef. But now he was gone and Yaakov was left alone in the world, with no one to bless or look after him.

"What shall I do?" Yankele begged the *hasidim*. "Isn't there anybody who can bless me? I need help fast."

They discussed it among themselves: "Talk to Rav Yaakov Yosef of Polonnoye. Many say he will succeed the holy Baal Shem."

Rav Yaakov Yosef was one of the three major pupils of the Baal Shem Tov and, maybe, next in line. We're not in a position to judge but, one thing's for sure, he was not the holy Baal Shem. For when Yankele came tearing into his *beis midrash*, shouting "Rebbe! Rebbe! Bless me fast!" Rav Yaakov Yosef's only response was one of suspicion.

"Fast? What do you mean?"

"I'm Yankele Ganef. I just stole fifty thousand rubles and the cops are hot on my trail. I need your blessing so they will forget the whole thing."

"Are you crazy? You're not ashamed to come into my synagogue and tell me you're a thief? To top it off, you want my blessing for your protection when you have committed a sin? Get out of here!"

Oy, gevalt! Obviously Reb Yaakov Yosef was not the holy Baal Shem Tov. With the police still hot on his trail, Yankele knew he had only one place to go. He ran straight to the cemetery and threw himself on the fresh grave of his holy master.

"Holy Baal Shem," he cried. "I see you left a rebbe for the *zaddikim* but how could you leave this world without appointing a rebbe for us thieves? For the broken and desperate of this world?"

Yankele cried bitterly because, let's face it . . . this was the end! What good were fifty thousand rubles going to do him in prison? He was so exhausted from his running and his crying that he fell asleep, stretched across the grave of the holy Baal Shem Tov.

Suddenly, his master appeared to him in a dream: "Yankele! Are you listening? I want you to know that, since the destruction of the Temple, no prayer shook Heaven like yours. Because it's so true. Everybody wants to be a rebbe of *zaddikim*, but who wants to take care of thieves? So I have come to tell you that I never forgot you for one second! I appointed my grandson, the *heilige* Degel Machane Ephraim of Sudylkow, to be the rebbe of all the holy thieves.

"Go to him! But in order for him to know that I sent you, I will teach you the Torah portion of the week—the way it is handed over in *Gan Eden*. Every Friday night I have been teaching my grandson the Torah from Paradise. If you can repeat it to him word for word, he'll understand it's a sign that I myself sent you."

And the holy Baal Shem gave Yankele a heavenly teaching. Yankele awoke from his dream. From Medzhibozh to Sudylkow was just a few kilometers. He took off at a fast run and arrived, breathless, at the door of the synagogue of the *heilige* Reb Ephraim.

"Rebbe! Please, I need to speak to you in private."

Reb Ephraim led him into his study, where Yankele began turning over to him, word for word, the Baal Shem Tov's secret teaching.

Reb Machane Ephraim was amazed. "Yaakov, how do you know this?"

"Your grandfather, my master, came back from Heaven to teach me this Torah as a sign that you should bless me. You see, I'm a thief. . . . " And Yankele told Reb Degel Machane Ephraim the whole story of the fifty thousand rubles.

Reb Degel Machane Ephraim blessed Yankele and, at about that time, the nobleman decided it was more important for him to press on to St. Petersburg than to chase after a common thief. So he left Medzibuhz without pressing charges and without his fifty thousand rubles.

The miracle of this story is that, after the Baal Shem Tov taught Yankele the Torah from Paradise, the thief could never steal again. While the holy Baal Shem was alive, he was only able to temper Yankele's nature but couldn't completely stop him from stealing. But when the holy master died and came back to Yankele from Heaven, with every word he taught him he was mamash *fixing his soul.*

The truth is that Yankele became a leading hasid of the heilige *Sudylkower to such a degree that Rav Degel Machane Ephraim made him a rebbe. And I'm sure that when Yaakov became a rabbi, he never forgot his fellow thieves. For by then he understood that, even the lowest sinner has some part of himself that is pure—that has nothing to do with his sin. It's the dream that someday he will become one of the highest* zaddiks *in the world.*

When Yankele started out in life, he didn't want to learn one page of Gemora*, then turn to the next. He wanted to know the deepest depths of truth. When he didn't achieve this at an early age, he turned away—not because he didn't love God or because he wanted to become evil. Only because he had given up.*

The Baal Shem Tov came along and gave him the guidance that would enable him to fulfill his dream. He protected Yankele, giving him time to realize his own holiness.

When the Messiah comes, we too will see . . . no mistake!! Our hopes aren't too exalted. We are really as holy as we dream.

The Wheel

Reb Yisroel Sadigorer was a rebbe for only a few years because, sadly enough, he passed away when he was still quite young. While alive, the rebbe had one *hasid*, Moishe, who was very devoted to him. Moishele was considered a very wealthy man and a strong supporter of the rebbe and his *hevrah*.

Now, some people are rich because they own, and others because they owe. Moishe's wealth was of the second variety: he seemed very rich but actually was on the verge of bankruptcy. One day, all of his creditors appeared at his door. Moishele was told he had exactly two weeks to raise two thousand rubles—in those days, a fortune—or he would be ruined.

On the day Moishe received this very bad news, he also received a letter from his holy master, Reb Yisroel Sadigorer. "In fourteen days I will need two thousand rubles to dower a poor bride. Please be so kind as to donate this money. To save time, I'd appreciate you bringing the money to me yourself, for the matter is quite urgent."

Upon considering the letter, it seemed to Moishe, as a firm believer in Reb Yisroel Sadigorer, that his luck was looking up. His logic went like this: "If on the same day I learn I'll be bankrupt unless I get two thousand rubles, I receive a letter from my rebbe requesting the same amount . . . somebody must be trying to tell me something." Since he couldn't raise four thousand rubles in two weeks, Moishe decided to listen to his rebbe and raise only the money for the bride.

"After all," he said to himself, "clearly, the merit I earn from the *mitzvah* of dowering a bride will protect me from bankruptcy."

He was so convinced that nothing bad would happen to his business that he told his frantic wife as he left the house, "Don't worry, Malkale. I got a letter from the rebbe. God is taking care of us."

And so, instead of attending to his affairs, Moishe went to outlying villages to collect from the other *hasidim*. On the thirteenth day, exactly one day before he was to go to the rebbe, he came home, *Baruch HaShem*, with two thousand rubles in his pocket. But when he reached his house, nobody was there. The house was stark empty. His family and furniture had been tossed out on the street. The bank had declared him bankrupt and, in his absence, confiscated his house. *Gevalt*! What should he do?

You know, sweetest friends, you may have many people close to you when you're in the money, but the moment you're poor. . . . It took Moishe all afternoon to dig up one *hasidishe yidele* kind enough to say, "I cannot let you move into my house, but if you want, you can use my stable."

Moishe was more than happy just to have a roof over his head. He moved his family and furniture into the stable, a temporary measure till he could get to his rebbe. But that night, there was a four-alarm fire and the whole stable burned down. Everything he owned was destroyed. He and his family barely escaped in their pajamas, and yet Moishe saved the two thousand rubles he had under his pillow.

Standing in the dark with next to nothing on, Moishe had a sudden doubt: "The rebbe knows everything. Why hasn't he protected me from all this calamity?" But still Moishe trusted the rebbe. Still he believed.

The next day, Moishe borrowed a *kapote* and a pair of pants and went to see the holy Sadigorer. In his mind, he was 100 percent sure that the minute he walked in the door the *heilige* Sadigorer would receive him royally, thank and bless him. His fortune would be restored. But when he walked into the rebbe's house and put the two thousand rubles on the table, the rebbe didn't say a word.

"*Gurnisht*! What's this? I sacrificed everything I owned for a poor bride I don't even know. . . . My wife and family have nothing and the rebbe can't even say hello?"

He pushed the money right under the rebbe's nose. Finally, finally, the rebbe looked up. "Thank you, Moishe," he said and started counting his rubles.

Moishele couldn't believe his eyes. He started respectfully backing away from the rebbe. But his heart was about to explode. What did the rebbe think? That this money came easily?

"Doesn't he know what I've been through? Either he doesn't know or he doesn't care."

When Moishele reached the door, he stopped. He didn't have time to be polite He marched straight back to the holy Reb Yisroel Sadigorer and shouted: "Rebbe, I want you to know, this is the last time you're ever going to see my face! I thought you could see from one corner of the world to the other, but now I know that you're only a fake! You didn't know that I'm now bankrupt, that I've lost everything—even the shirt on my back. You didn't care that my family has become destitute. All you wanted was for me to go around collecting these two thousand rubles!"

The Sadigorer pointed to a chair. "Moishele, sit down."

Moishele sat and the Sadigorer began to explain: "I want you to know that exactly what we are experiencing today happened to my holy grandfather, the holy Rizhyner, and one of his *hasidim*. My grandfather needed two thousand rubles for a poor bride. A *yidele*, one of his *hasidim*, came into the house and put the money on the table, expecting a miracle. He too had suffered exactly as you–from bankruptcy, loss of house, the stable burning until there was nothing left.

"When he handed over the money and the miracle didn't happen, the *hasid* started to walk out, then stopped and my grandfather, the holy Rizhyner, said: 'Yosele, sit down. I want to tell you a story.' This is what my grandfather told him":

Many years ago, there was a very wealthy merchant named Mendel David who was very skilled in business, but he had one *meshugas*, one craziness. He would never buy anything on credit. Every year he went to the fair in Leipzig and brought home millions in merchandise, for which he would only pay cash.

Mendel David had a little box in which he kept his millions. He and his most devoted friend, his trusted accountant, always traveled together to Leipzig and took turns guarding the chest.

Once, the two men decided to stop for a picnic in a beautiful spot on the outskirts of Leipzig before going into the town. It was the merchant's turn to watch the chest. He put the box under his hat and lay back on the grass, using the box as a headrest as he gazed up at the sky through the trees. The merchant was so moved by the beauty of the place that he completely forgot where he was.

"What a beautiful world God created for us," he sighed, and fell asleep. The accountant agreed with him, and they both dozed off. When they awoke, it was late. They jumped up and left in order to get to Leipzig before dark. Neither of them remembered the box. Nobody even so much as thought about the treasure until months later when it came time to pay for the merchandise Mendel David had selected.

"What splendid goods we've found in Leipzig this year," Mendel David said to his accountant. "Here's what I want you to pay . . ." and he handed him the list.

"Wait a minute!" the accountant cried. "Where's the money box?"

"The chest? I don't know. I thought you had it!"

"I? No. You had it with you while we were traveling so I assumed, once we reached Leipzig, you had put it away."

"No, I didn't touch it. I thought it was your turn to carry it."

Both men had forgotten when and where they

had last seen the box. Because they were such good friends, neither blamed the other. Instead each doubted himself. But they had a serious problem.

"*Gevalt*! We have to pay today! What are we going to do?"

Word of their calamity spread, and the merchants who had been doing business with Mendel David for years said, without hesitation:

"Mendel David! We trust you! Please, take our merchandise on credit and pay us back next year." But Mendel David refused, even though it meant he would end up with nothing.

The accountant tried to talk his friend out of his *meshugas*, for once, but Mendel David was convinced. So they left Leipzig without having bought a thing. Mendel David was very quiet and depressed, the accountant overcome with worry for his friend.

As they passed their picnic spot in the forest, they were again touched by its beauty. Mendel David said: "Do you remember the last time we were here? I was so wealthy and now I'm poor, like a dog. Let's make a stop for old times' sake."

He went to lie down on the grass, leaned his head back and struck against something hard. Can you believe—the chest was still there? After three months, a box with a million rubles was still waiting for them in a picnic spot frequented by thousands going to and from the fair!

When he opened the box and found all his monies intact, Mendel David broke down and cried. The accountant couldn't believe it: "Why are you crying? You should be beside yourself with joy! Don't you see? It's not too late! We still have time to go back to Leipzig and pick up our goods!"

Mendel David continued to weep uncontrollably. He couldn't stop. He reached into the box, took out half the money, and handed the accountant the chest. "Friend," he sobbed, "we've been together a long time, but now we must separate. Half this money is yours. Use it however you want, but leave me this instant!"

The accountant tried to persuade Mendel David that they should stay together, but it was as if Mendel David had lost his mind. The loss and recovery of his total fortune in one day had been too much of a shock for him.

So the accountant left.

Mendel David took the rest of the rubles and made his way home. He bought other merchandise with the money, but nothing of the quality he had seen in Leipzig, so it didn't sell. In a short amount of time, Mendel David lost all his remaining rubles and really went bankrupt. He was now out on the streets, a beggar.

As a beggar, Mendel David was too shy. He was so ashamed to be asking for money, he would never look anyone in the eye. Instead, he would cover his face with his arm and almost whisper: "Please give a poor man some money."

If you know anything about the profession of begging, this just doesn't go. A more aggressive beggar—who probably needed less but had a better sales pitch—would push him aside and get the money instead. So naturally, because of this shortcoming, Mendel David was, *mamash*, starving. Slowly, slowly he realized (if he were going to survive), he would have to join the *schnorers'* union. The captain of the union organized the beggars in teams and assigned each a different territory. The captain had all the inside information about the best places to beg. But since Mendel David was a newcomer, and obviously shy, the captain couldn't help being mean. He sent Mendel David to the most difficult place to beg.

Outwardly, of course, the captain was very nice to him. "Mendel David," he said, "we've decided to give you a break. For your introductory offer to our union, we're sending you to one of the richest, most generous men in town."

Mendel David knocked on the door. As soon as he heard the lock pulled back and the door open, he covered his eyes with his arm and held out his other hand.

"Please," he mumbled, "could you give some money to a poor soul?"

The rich man's eyes seemed to study him.

"Come in!" the owner of the house finally said. "You look tired. Are you thirsty?"

Mendel David timidly came into the alcove.

"Perhaps I could offer you something to drink."

Mendel David was quite surprised. No one had talked to him with such respect since he had been a successful merchant. He accepted a glass of tea, but the whole time he was drinking it, he covered his face with his arm.

The rich man took away the empty glass and said: "Perhaps you would do me the honor of staying for lunch."

Mendel David was starving. He hadn't eaten a good meal for months. "I'd be delighted." He sat down and ate, but the whole time he kept his eyes on the linen tablecloth and never once looked up.

When it came time to go, the rich man followed him to the door and pressed a gold piece into his hand. "Will you come back tomorrow for lunch?" the rich man asked.

"Yes. Yes." Mendel David nodded his head humbly, gave his thanks, and went on his way. This was Wednesday. Wednesday night, Mendel David came back to the *schnorers* union and told them the whole story, believing—as the captain had said—that the rich man was always so generous.

Unfortunately, men, particularly in low circumstances, can be quite greedy. These men were so jealous that Mendel David had succeeded where they had failed, they stole the gold ruble from his pocket while he was sleeping. As dues, they said.

When he awoke in the morning, Mendel David was so innocent, he thought he had lost the ruble somewhere along the way. He was so trusting that he became very upset with himself.

When Mendel David went back to the rich man's house for lunch, his host gave him another gold piece and said: "Friend, if you will be my guest for *Shabbes*, I'll give you one hundred gold rubles."

Mendel David couldn't believe his good fortune. He was so happy he went back to the *schnorers'* union and stupidly told the *schleppers* he'd been invited to the rich man's home for *Shabbes* and promised one hundred rubles.

The beggars were beside themselves with envy. They not only stole the gold piece out of his pocket, they decided to take revenge.

Every Friday afternoon, the *schnorers* would go to the *mikveh* to wash themselves. They'd sit and soak in the water and soap to make themselves presentable for some rich man's *Shabbes* table. Mendel David, who had once had a bathtub of his own, couldn't wait to wash himself clean. He felt so good in the water that he stayed a long time. But when he emerged, he discovered—to his horror—that his clothes were gone.

When a rich man yells for another suit, the valet jumps. But when a beggar starts screaming that someone has stolen his clothes, nobody seems to hear. Mendel David was crying, begging every man left in the *mikveh*: "People, please somebody, help me! Give me something, anything, to wear!"

Nobody paid any attention. Finally, the last *yidele* left the *mikveh*. At five minutes before *Shabbes* was to begin, the caretaker pushed Mendel David, naked, onto the street.

Okay. He's standing in front of the bathhouse. What does Mendel David do? He dashes across the street to the nearest tree and hides behind it, waiting for a miracle.

In those days, a man wouldn't think of sitting down at his *Shabbes* table without a poor man to share his feast. So the rich man was waiting for his poor guest. He wouldn't make *kiddush* without him. When Mendel David failed to appear, the rich man (who was obviously quite sensitive) feared something had happened to him.

He sent his children out to look for him, shouting after them as they left: "Go next door to the neighbor's and ask one of their *schnorer* guests. . . . Maybe they know where he is!"

The children knocked on the neighbor's door and asked an old grouch, who was sitting at the far end of the table and stuffing his face, "Have you seen the beggar who was supposed to come to our house for *Shabbes*?"

The *schnorer* laughed, a very nasty laugh. "Ha-ha. Yeah, I saw him."

"Where is he?"

"Probably still floating in the *mikveh*. Ha-ha-ha!"

The children took off at top speed, afraid, God forbid, that something had happened to the poor man. He might be locked in the bathhouse or have drowned. What did they see when they reached the *mikveh* but the *yidele*, naked as if he were in Paradise, dancing around a tree, and singing "*Kol Mekadesh Shvi'i*" at the top of his lungs! The children were astonished. They had never heard this *Shabbes zmirah* sung with such joy.

The oldest son threw his coat around Mendel David and brought him home for *Shabbes*. After having been seen naked, Mendel David was even more humiliated. Even though he was now dressed in a suit that his host had lent him, he still slumped. He ate with his arm over his eyes. His beard was almost in his soup. He never once dared to look at his host, through all three meals of *Shabbes*.

Finally, *Havdalah* came. *Shabbes* was over, the new week was ready to begin, and the rich man, as he handed Mendel David the hundred rubles, said to him: "You've spent all of *Shabbes* with me. Don't you think you could have the courtesy to face your host?"

His arm trembling, Mendel David took his hand away from his face. Who stood before him? His dear friend, the accountant.

The two men embraced and the accountant

said to Mendel David: "Brother! Master! At one time you gave me half of what you had. Now, *Baruch HaShem*, by investing what you gave me of your fortune, I've become richer than you ever were.

"I'll give you half of what is mine, if you'll explain to me why, when you found your money box, you wept as if it were the Destruction of the Temple. But when you had to hide outside the *mikveh* with nothing on, you sang as if it were Simhas Torah?"

"Everybody knows there's a wheel that governs our luck. When I lost my money box and found it again intact, I knew that I had reached the top of the wheel. From here on, I could only go down. Not wanting to drag you with me, I gave you a share of the money so you would be free.

"But when I became a beggar so poor that even the clothes on my back were stolen from me, I knew I had finally reached the bottom. From here on, I would be going up. So I danced and sang, because I am going up. What more is there to say, but "'*LeHaim*!'"

"And so," the holy Sadigorer explained to Moishe, "my grandfather, the *heilige* Rizhyner, said to the *yid* who brought him the two thousand rubles: 'There is a wheel that governs our *mazal*, our luck in this world.' I saw that you were on your way down and would have gone slowly bankrupt over the next ten years. For the *mitzvah* of giving your last cent to a poor bride, I knocked you all the way down so you could already begin to make your way back up again."

Then the holy Sadigorer blessed Moishe. And he said: "God should make you one hundred times richer than you were before as God owes you for giving your last money to the bride.

"But I say: Because you listened to me, Moishe, I'm going to take you off the wheel. From now on, you'll only go up."

This story is really about the Jewish people. When they came out of Egypt and built the first Temple, they wondered: How high can you reach? But when the Temple was destroyed and they were forced into exile, they found themselves in the lowest state.

And when, finally, they returned to Jerusalem to rebuild the Temple, can you imagine their joy—to have lost the Temple only to have it restored to them? And then, can you imagine the pain, when the Second Temple was destroyed and they went into exile again?

But this time, they say, "We're going to be taken off the wheel. When we go up, we're not coming down again."

You Must See What's After

There are many passages in the Torah, hasidic teachings and stories, that were not really meant for the generation in which they were originally told. Their full meaning can only be understood in later generations, once they have been lived. For example, our father Yaakov said, when he awoke from the dream: "Please, God, give me bread to eat and clothes to wear."

Yaakov Avinu was praying that the Jewish people should never have to give their food for a shirt, their shirt for food. The Chabina Rav, one of the great scholars to survive the Second World War, saw the importance of this prayer. For in Auschwitz, people would give their shirt for a piece of bread. While in Siberia, they gave their bread for a shirt. In tragedies like these, having bread to eat and clothes to wear saved the Jewish people from destruction.

This same principle is true also of a story I heard in 1948 when I was studying at the yeshivah *in Lakewood. It was announced that the chief rabbi of Persia was coming to visit us. I, like most of the students, expected the chief rabbi of Persia to be a Sephardic Jew. But when I walked into the room to meet him, I saw a* yidele *with a* streimel, mamash, *a Belzer* hasid.

That Shabbes *I had the privilege of spending most of the day alone with this rabbi. He recounted many stories as we walked around Lakewood, but this one has always been the clearest in my mind. He had first heard the tale from his grandfather many years before the War. When his* zeide *first told him the story, the old man took his grandson's hand and made him promise to tell the story to others, especially on Saturday night.*

"Always," his zeide *used to say, "you must take hold of your listener's hand." So the chief rabbi of Persia took my hand and asked that I make the same promise to him. When I heard the story, I understood how prophetic his* zeide*'s story had been. Because, although first told years before, it was really the story of the Six Million.*

In a village not far from Lyzhansk lived a *yidele*, an innkeeper named Moishele. "Moishele," they called him, "Moishele the *cretchmir*." Business wasn't always so great. Like many of the *yidden* in those times, there were sometimes months when Moishe couldn't pay his rent. As I've told you before, if you couldn't pay the rent when the landlord came around to collect it, you had to run for your life! Because the landlord could kill you, take your wife and children to sell as slaves, maybe even kill them as well.

As Moishele hadn't paid the rent for several months, his landlord decided to foreclose. The nobleman appeared one morning at the door of the *cretchmir*, walked in and said, "Moishele, if you don't pay up by Monday, I'm going to kill you for sure."

Moishele was in a panic, but his wife was a woman of faith. "Don't be afraid, Moishele. I've heard there's an incredible *yid* in Lyzhansk, Reb Elimelech. Go to him! Write on a slip of paper what you need, and he will help you."

Moishele was exceedingly poor. He had shoes, but he didn't want to wear out the soles, so he tied the strings together and slung them over his shoulder. As he was almost illiterate, he took a big piece of paper and scribbled a sign in large letters that said: "Rav Elimelech. I need money for the rent."

Wearing the shoes on his back, the sign over his heart, Moishele walked to Lyzhansk. On his way he met all the holy *hasidim* like the Seer of Lublin, Reb Mendele of Vitebsk, and the Roptchitzer. The Lubliner, when he saw Moishe, said to him: "Hey, *foigel*! Little crazy bird! Where are you going?"

"To Lyzhansk to see Reb Elimelech. He's going to give me money for the rent!"

The Lubliner said: "Let me see the letter you wrote him."

Moishele was embarrassed because of his spelling, but upon persuasion let the holy Lubliner have a look. But, as you know, the Seer of Lublin was no ordinary reader. When he looked at the letter, he knew that the landlord really meant to kill Moishele. So he cautioned the *cretchmir*:

"Moishele, promise me that Monday you'll go into hiding!"

Moishele was furious. "I'm not interested in your advice, only in what Reb Elimelech has to say!"

And, lonely and barefoot, he continued on his way to Lyzhansk. The others followed to see what would happen.

At Reb Elimelech's door, Moishele slipped on his shoes and knocked. Once invited, he opened the door and shouted: "Melek, give me money for the rent!"

Reb Elimelech took Moishele's *kvittel*, his written request, off his chest and read: "Rav Elimelech. I need money for the rent."

As Reb Elimelech read the petition, he saw not only the letters painted on the page, but the faces of all those who had read it before him. So Reb Elimelech knew that the Seer of Lublin had already given his advice to the *cretchmir*.

"Moishele," Reb Elimelech counseled him. "Tell the nobleman that if he wants you to stay, he will have to give you ten thousand rubles."

What's this? Moishele owes his landlord rent and he's supposed to *charge* the nobleman an unbelievable sum for the privilege of keeping the *cretchmir* as his tenant? Moishele started yelling at the rebbe: "Melek! Are you crazy? I tell you the man intends to kill me if I don't pay the rent, and you come out with this nonsense! Make yourself crazy, but leave me alone!"

And he took off his shoes and *schlepped* back to his village. When Moishele got home to his wife, he threw his shoes on the table and yelled at her. "Maybe the man was once very great, but your Reb Elimelech is senile. An idiot!" And not knowing what else to do or where else to go, Moishele put the whole matter out of his mind. In fact, he completely forgot that the landlord intended to kill him on Monday morning.

Monday, Moishe was walking down the street, when the nobleman rode over to him. "So, Moishele, where's my money?"

Moishele shrugged. "I don't have it."

The nobleman got off his horse and beat Moishele with his whip, then and there. Moishele was barely alive, unable to move. Blood was pouring off his brow. Finally, thinking Moishele was dead, the landlord galloped off again. Moishele began to crawl home on all fours. Needless to say, he was very sorry he hadn't listened to the holy Lubliner's advice to hide on Monday.

Now even the greatest anti-Semite has one Jew he cares for. The nobleman's wife adored Moishele. Without him, she could not function in the marketplace. "Moichik," she called him, because Moishele always made bargains for her.

The nobleman's wife had been riding about the square looking for Moishele but couldn't find him anywhere. Greatly distressed, she asked her husband that day: "Have you seen my Moichik?"

"Your Moichik is dead. I knocked him off an hour ago for not paying the rent."

"What? If you want to kill a Jew, pick on somebody else but don't you touch my Moichik," the nobleman's wife cried. She was so upset that she began hitting her husband. "He'd better not be dead. Wherever he is, you'd better find and revive him."

So the nobleman went searching for Moishele. He followed the trail of blood from the place of attack to the inn. Moishele, hearing the landlord's horse approaching, barricaded himself in the inn, thinking the man meant to finish him off.

"I didn't listen to the Seer of Lublin this morning when he told me to hide," Moishele groaned, greatly in pain. "But I'll do it now!"

When the landlord knocked, Moishele wouldn't open. He didn't make a sound. Instead he lay, shivering from fright, under a pile of old blankets, awaiting the end.

The nobleman banged on the door, calling: "Moishele, are you alive? Are you in there? Moishele, Moishele, I swear! I won't hurt you anymore. I came to make up! My wife wants you to stay and take care of the *cretchma*!"

When Moishele heard this, he remembered suddenly the advice Reb Elimelech had given him, crazy as it had seemed. He crept to the door and listened carefully as the landlord repeated his offer a second time.

"I'll only stay if you give me ten thousand rubles to build up my business again," Moishele answered him.

"Anything! Just come out so I can make sure you're all right!"

The nobleman gave Moishele a loan and between innkeeping and bargaining in the marketplace, Moishe's business became a great success. In fact, he became rich.

After about a year, his wife said to him: "You know, Moishele. Reb Elimelech really did help you, even though you were so rude to him. Yet you've never gone back to thank him."

So they went to Lyzhansk, only this time Moishele not only had shoes, he had a horse and wagon like a genuine merchant. When he arrived at the home of Reb Elimelech, who also was there at the time? The Seer of Lublin, Reb Mendele of Vitebsk, and the Roptchitzer rebbe. Even in his fancy dress, the four rebbes recognized Moishele from the year before.

"Moishele, you've come back! Tell us what happened to you with the rent!"

After Moishele had recounted his story, Reb Elimelech turned to the Seer of Lublin and said: "You see! And I see! You saw only as far as the beating, but I saw what came after."

When he finished the tale, the chief rabbi of Persia told me: "At first, I couldn't understand why my grandfather was so eager to have me promise to tell this story to everyone I met, especially on Saturday night. But after the Holocaust, I began to understand the reason. We must see what's after, if we are to survive and build ourselves back up again."

The Grave Next to the Megale Amukos

One of the most exalted kabbalists in the world was the Megale Amukos. "Megal Amukos" means Revealer of the Depths. When this sage passed away, sometime between 1620 and 1660, he was considered so holy that nobody was allowed to be buried next to him. A large area was left around his grave in the cemetery of Cracow, never to be used.

A century after his death, a poor *yidele* knocked late one night on the door of the president of the synagogue of Cracow. In those days, the president was in charge of burial plots in the cemetery for the entire Jewish community. The stranger, a Jew to be sure, stood on the threshold of the president's house and said:

"Here is a hundred rubles. I want to be buried next to the Megale Amukos."

Half asleep at the time, the president of the *shul* thought at first the man was joking. No one in the world could expect to be buried next to the Megale Amukos, much less this *schlepper*. But then, sensing the stranger's seriousness, he began to fear the man might be crazy.

So the president thought to himself: "Better I should take the money and give it to the poor than argue with this man."

He accepted the money, put it in a drawer and went back to sleep. The next morning, during prayers, there was a commotion in the synagogue. Someone had died in the middle of *davening*. The president, called to attend, immediately recognized the beggar whose money he had taken the night before.

"Clearly this *schlepper* knew enough to know he was going to die," the president thought to himself.

But he couldn't bring himself to bury the beggar in the plot next to the Megale Amukos. Rather, he said nothing about the whole affair. After all, the man was dead. Besides, how was he going to explain to the community that he had sold their most precious gravesite for a hundred rubles?

Since nobody knew the beggar, he was buried in the cemetery for the poor on the other side of the graveyard and the hundred rubles was given to charity.

But the story does not end here: there are those who are simply poor *schleppers* and then there's the hidden. That night, the beggar appeared to the president in his dream.

"I'm calling you before the Heavenly Court," he said accusingly, "if you don't bury me in the grave I bought next to the Megale Amukos."

The president awoke, relieved to find it was only dream, and did nothing.

The second night, the beggar came again in his sleep. By the third night, the *schlepper* was threatening. "Mr. President, this is no joke! Either you bury me where I belong or I'll bring you up to heaven with me."

Which meant, of course, that the president would die.

First thing in the morning, the president ran to the rabbi. I don't know who the chief rabbi of Cracow was at that time, but the chief rabbis were always noted kabbalists. The president told the Rabbi the whole story and was reprimanded immediately.

"You had no right to go back on your deal! You shouldn't have taken the hundred rubles in the first place, but once you did, the beggar owned the gravesite, fair and square."

"What shall I do? He intends to kill me and take me before the Heavenly Court. But I can't just bury him in that gravesite. Everyone will be on top of me with their questions: Why him? Why not me?"

"Listen, when the beggar returns tonight, ask him to do you one favor. Say you're not ready yet to be judged in heaven, but you are willing to be called before the living court, the *beis din*. He should appear tomorrow morning, ten o'clock, in the *beis midrash* and a decision will be given."

You would really have to be an extraordinary kabbalist to handle a case like this. Obviously, the rabbis of Cracow were on such a level. For when the Court was convened, the rabbi took a *tallit* and, placing it on a chair, designated the place where the soul of the beggar should sit. Then he called out to him.

"Holy beggar, state your case!"

"I bought the grave for a hundred rubles. The president accepted my money. It's now mine."

The president started blustering. "It's absurd! How can anyone dream of being buried next to the Megale Amukos, much less of buying the grave next to him for a hundred rubles? It's one of the holiest places in the world."

The holy court of Cracow gathered together, and this was their decision:

"Beggar, we're not on the level to know if you're holy enough to be buried next to the Megale Amukos. But one thing is clear: If you *are* worthy, you don't need our help to get you there."

The next morning, the beggar's plot in the poor man's cemetery was found empty, and a fresh mound had appeared next to the Megale Amukos. This story is so true that you can visit the tombstone. But as the rabbis never knew the beggar's name, they could only write on the marker:

"Here lies the unknown *zaddik*."

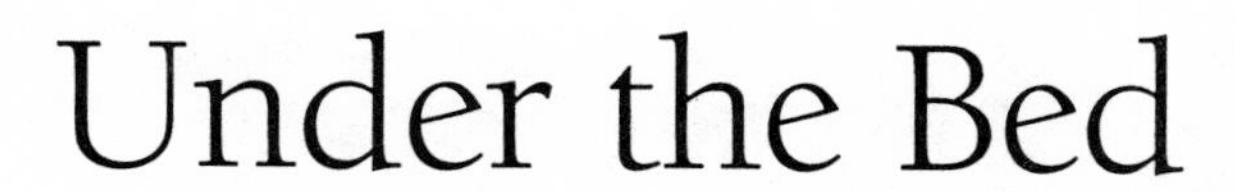

Under the Bed

Most people are so out of touch with life in this world that they think it's crazy to speak of life on the Other Side. But it isn't. There's life in this world and the next. According to Jewish tradition, while Heaven is more pure, life in this world is the central focus. Men come here to be fixed and made whole.

Word has it that the zaddikim *run both worlds. Essentially, they run the whole show. The Heavenly Court is governed by* zaddikim *who have died recently. They replace other righteous men,* zaddikim *who've been in Heaven too long to remember the reality of struggle in this world.*

Once Rav Michel Zlotchever passed away, he was called to judge on the Heavenly Court. As soon as he took his place, he came down harshly on all those he had to review.

"How could you do such wrong?" he yelled at them.

Finally, one of the zaddikim *on earth realized what was happening and began to complain: "You can't appoint, as a judge, a man who has never sinned! What does the Zlotchever know of the hardships of Moishe the Water Carrier? He comes from a family that for thirteen generations made no mistakes."*

The worldly zaddikim *protested his severity so much that it was finally decreed that the Zlotchever would be retired and the* zaddik *who had first complained should take his place. The decree went out just before* Shabbes. *The* zaddik *on earth barely had enough time to say good-bye to his wife.*

Judging is done in heaven, but fixing takes place in this world—sometimes before the Judgment, sometimes after. We are speaking here of fixing the souls of those who have left this world. Judging will determine whether you go to Heaven or Hell, whether you are permitted to come back to life.

But if the merchandise is damaged, it's not a question of Paradise or reincarnation. The vessels are broken. They need to be mended and made whole again. This kind of repair doesn't take place in Heaven. Nor can we do it ourselves.

A soul who needs fixing has to come back into the world and look for a zaddik *to help him. Naturally, if he was close to one while he was alive he will have no problem, because his soul is still attached to that* zaddik. *But what happens to a person who was never attached to a* zaddik *during his lifetime?*

verybody knows that the Trisker Maggid, Rav Avromole, was one of the eight sons of Reb Motele Chernobyl who was *mamash* a *zaddik gadol*. Rav Motele was the center of all the *zaddikim*. He took care of the living and the dead and was the master of the *lamed-vav zaddikim*, the Thirty-Six Righteous Men who hold up the world.

Before he passed away, Reb Motele divided his kingdom among his children and put the Trisker Maggid in charge of the people from the Other Side.

Rav Avromole lived like this. Eight o'clock in the morning he'd get up, go to the *mikveh*, pray. Two o'clock in the afternoon, he would start to yawn. "I'm so tired, I've got to lie down a little bit." He'd go to his room until three, then pray both afternoon and evening prayers. Ten o'clock at night he might start yawning again. "I'm so tired. I've got to go back to my room."

The fact of the matter is that the Trisker Maggid never ate and never slept. He also never kept any books in his room, because—as everybody knows—when he closed the door to his room he was dealing with souls from the Other World who needed fixing.

People from the Other Side are not able to read Torah. In order to avoid making them feel bad, the Trisker Maggid never permitted books in his room. If he found one, he put it out.

The Trisker Maggid once came to a village where only one *yidele* had enough room in his house to accommodate the rebbe and his *hasidim*. But this man was a real *misnagid*. He had heard many stories from his fellow *misnagdim* and was suspicious of the rumor that the Trisker Maggid never slept and never ate.

"Eating I can believe. He sleeps so much, he doesn't need to eat. But he doesn't even keep a book in his room, so you can't tell me he isn't up there napping!"

This wealthy *yidele* was more than happy to have the Trisker Maggid as his guest, because it would give him a chance to prove what Rav Avromole was doing behind closed doors. "He's snoring, I'm sure."

While the Trisker Maggid was *davening Maariv*, the evening prayer, the *yidele* managed to get into Rav Avromole's room and to hide under the bed.

At ten o'clock, the Trisker Maggid said to his *hasidim*, "I have to go back to my room."

The rich *yidele* heard Rav Avromole come into the chamber and felt him sit down on the bed.

No sooner had the *hasidim* closed the door to give the rebbe a little privacy when it seemed to open again. A crowd pushed their way into the room. The man could hear the shuffle of feet, the murmuring appeals.

During the day, the host had already witnessed the Trisker Maggid's audiences with ten, maybe even thirty people, at a time. But this sounded like thousands. What was happening? Where were all these people coming from? How could there even be a place for them in this little bedroom?

During the day, people would complain: "Rabbi! I'm sick. Please cure my back."

"I need money for my business."

"Would you find a wife for my son?"

But by night, the people were saying, "Rebbe! I'm so broken! They won't let me into Paradise. They won't let me into Hell. All I can do is wander. Rebbe, please fix my soul."

The worst was that the *misnagid* heard so many voices in the room. But when he peeked out from underneath the bed, he couldn't see any feet. The *yidele* was so frightened that he was shaking and had to do his best to keep his teeth from chattering.

Suddenly, he heard another, different voice cry out: "Rebbe! Have compassion on my tormented *neshamah*. Fix me! Fix my soul!"

"What can I do for you?" the Trisker Maggid asked. "While you were alive, you never bothered to come to me. You didn't even give me one penny *tzedakah*, one penny for charity, to connect yourself to me. So how can I help you now?"

"There must be a way!" The poor soul pleaded with the rebbe, from a place of deep anguish.

"Actually, there is one way. Your neighbor, Shmuelik, was one of my top *hasids*. Shmuelik gave me a great deal of charity during his lifetime. If he were to tell me now that one penny of the riches he gave as *tzedakah* was for you, then I could find a way to help you."

"Shmuelik would do that for me, I'm sure."

"Fine! Then I want you to go and ask him!"

"How can I do that? He won't believe that I come from you!"

"Then I'll send somebody along to act as your witness." At this point, the Trisker Maggid gave a strong, swift kick under the bed and said to the *yidele*: "Come out!"

When the *yidele* realized that the Trisker Maggid was about to send him into the Other World as witness to an exchange between two souls, he began pleading from under the bed. "Please, Rebbe! Don't do this to me! I promise I won't tell anybody what I saw!"

"Come out!"

The *yidele* came out, crawling on his stomach. He was crying, screaming, clinging to the rebbe's feet.

"Please, Rebbe! You've seen! I have a wife and three children. I don't want to die yet. I'm not ready to die!"

"God forbid you should die. But if you're going to spy on me, you must go as my witness. Take my stick and walk with the soul of this man to the cemetery."

The *yidele* looked around. The greatest nightmare of all was that there was absolutely no one else in the room, only himself and the Trisker Maggid.

"Knock on the first grave in the second row and say that Avrom ben Hannah orders Shmuel ben Rivkah to give one penny to fix the *neshamah* of this *yidele*—Yosele, his neighbor."

The beautiful aspect of this story is that I actually heard it from the great-great-grandson of the man who hid under the bed. It goes without saying that he lived to become a very great Trisker hasid.

Fixing the Exile

Dov Baer, the Mezhirech Maggid, once wrote to the Maggid of Mezhirech, Rav Abraham Joshua Heschel, the Apter Rebbe: "Don't force my holy pupil, Reb Zussia, to become a rebbe, because he's already beyond that." I'm sure these words have many interpretations, but here is one story that helps explain what he meant.

or two years, the Rebbe Reb Zussia and his brother, Rav Elimelech, walked around to "fix the exile." According to Judaism, God and His *Shechinah*, His Presence, are in exile. To understand their suffering, we too should taste something of that exile.

On another level, the Rebbe Reb Zussia and Rav Elimelech chose to get to know the world, because they knew you can sit over a book for a hundred years, but it may never compare to what you learn in one day walking down the street.

Of course, a Jew who wanders must always find a place to spend *Shabbes*. The brothers seemed to have no difficulty in this for every Thursday night their father would come to them in a dream and tell them where to pray for *Shabbes* and with whom to eat.

One particular weekend, as they were approaching a certain city, their father came from the Other World and said to Reb Elimelech: "This week, I want you to eat in the house of the rabbi."

But to the Rebbe Reb Zussia he said: "Zussia, I want you to eat with the shoemaker."

Rav Elimelech went to the rabbi's house and spent *Shabbes* there. Everything was in order, but there's nothing really to repeat. The Rebbe Reb Zussia went to the shoemaker's and the man wouldn't let him in the door.

"I know about people like you. You complain when you *daven*, and for good reason. Your *davening* is four hours long. It takes you ten years to get your food down your throat. I work hard all week. When I *daven* on *Shabbes*, I *daven* fast. I eat quickly and go to sleep. I don't want anybody in the house taking away from my rest."

The Rebbe Reb Zussia, who had a feeling that the shoemaker was a very special man, did his best to be welcomed. "I'll do everything you do, I swear. I'll *daven* fast, eat quickly, sleep. You'll have no complaints."

The shoemaker agreed, but only after he'd warned the Rebbe Reb Zussia. "If you don't keep your word, I'll throw you out in the middle of *Shabbes*."

Friday night they went to pray. The Rebbe Reb Zussia soon realized that there were only *lamed-vav zaddikim* praying with the shoemaker. They *davened* so fast that one of the Rebbe Reb Zussia's blessings took longer than their whole service. After five minutes, their prayers were finished. They went back to the shoemaker's home for a feast and, as his host had warned him, they ate in a flash. Before the Rebbe Reb Zussia had time to settle down, they were already giving thanks for their food.

The Rebbe Reb Zussia was so sure the shoemaker would be doing something special Friday night that he sat up all night, waiting for the shoemaker to rise. But while the Rebbe Reb Zussia was keeping watch, the shoemaker really slept. The next morning, the Rebbe Reb Zussia could barely wake up in time for prayers, which again lasted only a few minutes. The second meal they also ate in record time.

After giving thanks for the food, the shoemaker stood up, stretched, and yawned. "I'm going to sleep."

The Rebbe Reb Zussia also went and lay down, only this time he slept. When he woke up, there was nobody in the house. Everybody seemed to be away. He wandered about until he found a little boy.

"Where's your father and mother? Where's everyone?" Zussia asked.

The boy pointed upward. "They're in the attic for the third meal." The Rebbe Reb Zussia ran upstairs, only to find that the ladder to the attic had been pulled up so he couldn't join them.

So the Rebbe Reb Zussia went outside and climbed a tree. Nobody knows quite how he managed, but he soon found himself hanging by one hand from the roof and swinging while he peered through the attic window.

The Rebbe Reb Zussia looked and saw thirty-six families seated around a table, eating and learning. The shoemaker was sitting at the head of the table with his back to the Rebbe Reb Zussia. It gave the Rebbe Reb Zussia the shivers to think that he had been spending *Shabbes* in the home of the head of the thirty-six righteous men who held up the world.

The Rebbe Reb Zussia's hanging by one hand, afraid to fall but not wanting to miss a thing, when those nearest the window saw him. They began to protest: "Tell him to get down! He doesn't belong here!"

But when the shoemaker turned around and saw the Rebbe Reb Zussia hanging in the window, he said: "I can't. He's my guest. I can't just throw him out."

"Then let him in!"

So the shoemaker opened the window and the Rebbe Reb Zussia climbed into the attic, where he joined the thirty-six families for the third meal of *Shabbes*.

"I'm letting you in because I accepted you as my guest, but you must swear to me now that whatever you see or hear . . . you will tell no one." Because the *torahs* that the *lamed-vav zaddikim* tell each other are not for this world.

The Rebbe Reb Zussia swore. Obviously, he spent the highest Third Meal of his life. The Rebbe Reb Zussia stayed for the meal and then left the shoemaker's house with his heart—and his soul—on fire.

The next morning, the Rebbe Reb Zussia met up with Reb Elimelech and they went together to the synagogue to pray. Rav Elimelech soon realized that the Rebbe Reb Zussia's *davening* that day was something extraordinary. The Rebbe Reb Zussia was praying the way he—Reb Elimelech—might pray on Yom Kippur.

"What happened to you this *Shabbes*? Your praying is incredible. I feel as if you've climbed up the ladder two million miles and I'm left far behind."

The Rebbe Reb Zussia replied. "Nothing happened. It was an ordinary *Shabbes*."

"Tell me about the shoemaker."

The Rebbe Reb Zussia shrugged. "Nothing special. Just a shoemaker."

Reb Elimelech realized that the Rebbe Reb Zussia was hiding something from him. "Zussia, listen to me! When we set out together in the world, we promised to share everything. We swore to each other. You swore to me. I'm holding you to that promise."

The Rebbe Reb Zussia realized that he had indeed sworn to Reb Elimelech, long before his encounter with the shoemaker, that he would share all his experiences. As a second vow cannot annul the first, the Rebbe Reb Zussia decided that he must tell his brother everything–and did so.

That night, the two brothers came to a little inn. Since they were poor people, they slept as usual under the table. In the middle of the night, there was a heavy banging on the door. A nobleman entered, dressed in armor, his visor over his face. He asked the innkeeper, "Have you a good room where I can sleep?"

The innkeeper said, "For you, a nobleman, of course. I have the best."

As the innkeeper was leading him upstairs, the nobleman spotted the two brothers sleeping under the table. "Who are those two men?"

"They're two rabbis with no money to pay."

"I'll pay for them."

"But we have no more rooms."

"Make a bed for them in my room. I can't stand to see good people sleeping on the floor."

It was crazy: Reb Elimelech and the Rebbe Reb Zussia were awakened and brought into the room upstairs. The nobleman lay on the bed in his armor. They only had time to say "thank you very much" before they all went off to sleep. In the morning, the nobleman woke up very early and left. But after an hour, he returned, still in his armor. "Where are those two Jews? One of them stole my watch."

The innkeeper was very upset. "I don't believe it! They look like two very honest people."

"I don't care what you think. One of them stole!" The nobleman walked back to his room and grabbed the Rebbe Reb Zussia by the collar. "Did you steal my watch?"

The Rebbe Reb Zussia said: "No! I didn't steal your watch!"

The nobleman gave him a slap across his face. "Jew, confess! You stole!"

But the Rebbe Reb Zussia insisted. "I didn't. I didn't steal."

The nobleman hit him hard across the mouth. "Confess! Confess that you stole!"

Then the nobleman took Reb Elimelech, smacked him across the face, and said: "Confess you're the one! You stole my watch!"

When neither would confess, he chained them both to his wagon and whipped his horses. "I'm taking you both to the judge."

And he dragged them away. The Rebbe Reb Zussia and Reb Elimelech, after their beating, had little strength left. They barely made it to the judge, a nobleman like the first, in armor and visor.

The first nobleman said: "One of these two Jews, maybe both, stole my watch."

The judge ordered: "Confess that you stole."

"No!"

Bang. He knocked the two brothers to the ground.

After this, however, the two armored men left Rav Elimelech alone. Instead they began knocking off the Rebbe Reb Zussia, but nobody knew why.

The Rebbe Reb Zussia was *mamash* at his end.

The nobleman and judge announced: "This is your last chance. Do you confess or not?"

Zussia cried out: "I did not steal from you. Why do you keep accusing me?"

The nobleman and judge took off their visors, the Rebbe Reb Zussia recognized the shoemaker and one other of the *lamed-vav zaddikim.*

"Today, for breaking your vow to us, you were supposed to die. We prayed all night that you could escape with just a beating. So from now on, keep your vow. Because if you ever say another word about us to anybody, Zussia, you will die instantly!"

Everybody knows that the Rebbe Reb Zussia never said Torah after that, because the torahs *that he would have given over were not for this world. Which is why the Mezhirecher Maggid wrote to his pupil the Apter Rebbe: "Don't force Zussia to become a rebbe, because he's already beyond that."*

The Rich Man and the Thief

verybody knows that the Yid HaKadosh, the Holy Jew, was one of the highest pupils of the Seer of Lublin. The holy Lubliner wasn't rich, but he was a great rebbe, so he lived like a *mensch*. The Yid HaKadosh was very poor. He was dependent on his father-in-law, a humble baker who worked hard all week, to feed those in his household.

One Friday afternoon, the Yid HaKadosh came to see the Seer of Lublin in his only shirt, which was torn and badly in need of washing. For a *talmid hocham*, a scholar, to walk around dirty is a desecration of God's name. When the holy Lubliner saw the Yehudi HaKadosh in such a state, he had compassion on him.

"My friend, I can't let you go into *Shabbes* looking like this."

He went into his drawer and brought out a beautiful shirt, which he gave to the Holy Jew.

In our tradition, garment and soul are one. The holy Seer of Lublin—who had prophetic vision—would never have given one of his shirts to another man unless that man was very holy. So for the Yid HaKadosh to receive this gift from his teacher was the highest honor in the world. Unfortunately, the Yid HaKadosh was so filled with humility, he thought the Seer of Lublin only gave him the shirt because he needed one.

In those days, every poor man in town went to the *mikveh* late Friday afternoon to take a bath and scratch off the dirt from the week. The Yid HaKadosh thanked his teacher for the shirt and went off to the *mikveh*, to wash. On his way, he ran into Hatzkele the *shicker*, the drunkard. And he noticed immediately that Hatzkele's shirt was even more torn, more disreputable, than his own.

The Yid HaKadosh thought to himself: "I wish, just once, Hatzkele would look decent on *Shabbes*." Impulsively, he held out the shirt to the drunkard. "Here, Hatzkele! Want a good shirt? I just got this from the Seer of Lublin but I'm giving it to you—for *Shabbes*."

As I've told you before, there are those who drink for themselves, those who drink for all the Jews of a town, and a few superdrunkards who drink for all the Jews of the world since the time of Abraham. Hatzkele was not a superdrunkard, but he certainly drank for all of Lublin.

As his mind was only on drinking, Hatzkele didn't care about *Shabbes*. When the Holy Jew gave him the Lubliner's shirt, he ran straight to the *cretchma* and said to those hanging around: "Who's offering me the most for the shirt of the Seer of Lublin?"

He took bids from everyone in the bar. Finally, the bartender called out: "I'll give you free drinks for the whole year." Hatzkele gave him the shirt, thinking he had received the better part of the deal.

But Hatzkele underestimated the *cretchmir*. Monday, the bartender went to the marketplace, stood on a chair and shouted for all to hear: "I have in my hand the shirt of the Seer of Lublin! This shirt can give you every miracle known to mankind. Women who don't have children will conceive the minute their husbands put on this shirt! Women having a difficult pregnancy will give birth even before the full nine months!" Within twenty minutes of bargaining, the bartender had sold the shirt for ten thousand rubles.

The Holy Lubliner soon heard about the affair. I don't want to say anything bad, but he was mad that his gift had turned into such a low commercial deal. But more than feeling angry, the Holy Lubliner was hurt that the Yid HaKadosh should think so little of himself.

Gossip quickly reached the Yid HaKadosh that the Lubliner was angry. The Holy Jew felt terrible. He realized that a great wall had come between himself and his rebbe because he hadn't understood the true intention of the gift.

For the first time in his life, the Yid HaKadosh began to doubt his every deed. Totally ashamed of himself, he ran out of town. But where could he go without his rebbe? He sat down on a rock by the side of the road and wept.

Everybody knows that when a worthy person is truly broken, only one being can lift him up, and that is Eliyahu HaNovi, Elijah the Prophet. Because when a Jew is broken, he wants real answers, not just a pat on the head. In this case, Eliyahu HaNovi did not appear to the Holy Jew like the chief rabbi of I-know-not-where. He came like a drunkard, tottering down the street, sat down on the ground next to the Yid HaKadosh and put his hand on his shoulder.

"Hey, brother! What's the problem? Why are you crying?"

The Yehudi HaKadosh recounted the tale of the shirt. "For the first time in my life, it seems to me that all my good deeds only served to further the Other Side."

"Yehudi, you should never regret that out of the goodness of your heart, you gave the Lubliner's shirt to Hatzkele the Drunkard. After all, you never know how he might repay you someday."

When the Yid HaKadosh looked surprised, the Prophet added: Take my friends Avrom and Zev, for instance, who were neighbors over a century ago. Zev was a thief. He was such a professional that he could clean out a pocket, a purse, an entire house in the presence of his host without getting caught. The townspeople became progressively poorer, and Zev, proportionately rich.

Eventually, Zev became so established that it was beneath his dignity to steal. So he retired, bought himself a beautiful villa, and proceeded to enjoy his wealth. The only trouble with his retirement plan was that a thief who stops stealing has no more income. So Zev soon spent his monies, found he had nothing left and, like any poor beggar, went to the community to request some financial relief.

"Please! I'm suddenly so poor. Couldn't you give me a little bit of charity?"

"*Hutzpah*!" the townspeople yelled at him. "You give us back all the money you stole from us and we'll give you a little *tzedakah*."

There was nothing Zev could do. He no longer had any desire to steal, yet he knew no other trade by which to support himself. So he starved.

One Friday, Avrom, Zev's wealthy neighbor, was walking home from the *mikveh*. He noticed the ex-thief sitting on the stoop of his villa, looking downcast and completely broken.

"No matter what my neighbor did in the past,

I'm not going to let him starve on *Shabbes*!" Avrom said to himself. So he hurried home to his wife and had her prepare food for his neighbor, the thief, enough for all three meals of *Shabbes*. His wife, being a very good woman, prepared food not only for *Shabbes* but the rest of the week as well.

In this manner, Zev the Thief survived. It became a ritual. Every Friday, Avrom the Rich Man would send two packages off to his neighbor, one for *Shabbes* and the other for the rest of the week.

Three years later, both Avrom the Rich Man and Zev the Thief died, on the same day and at the same moment, in fact. Two funeral processions were held simultaneously. The whole city turned out to honor Avrom the Rich Man, but his neighbor the thief had only a few stray thieves who got together for old time's sake and walked behind the coffin.

Both Avrom the Rich Man and Zev the Thief went up to heaven. The rich man went before the Heavenly Court first. Everybody knows that in heaven one is judged before an immense scale. One side of the scale is for good deeds, the other for mistakes. So the Angel Michael came with his briefcase, pulled out Avrom's few good deeds, and personally put them on the scale. It took only a second; the scale barely moved.

Then Satan moved in, hauling ten wagon loads of bad deeds, which he proceeded to dump on the scale.

Avrom was in a sweat. He saw that his good deeds had absolutely no weight! God forbid, but obviously he could forget having a place in Paradise. Avrom was so frightened, he closed his eyes in order not to see the heavenly judges push a button and make him fall, like a barbecue into Hell.

Suddenly, he heard magnificent trumpets as the angels cried out in unison: "Avrom the Rich Man is to enter Paradise!"

"What's this?" Avrom opened his eyes, surely there had been a mistake.

Something was wrong with the scale: it was now tilted the other way. His few good deeds far outweighed the bad.

"What's going on here? What happened to all my sins?" he cried in confusion.

The angels laughed.

"Sins! The second you closed your eyes, your friend Zev the Thief crept up behind you and stole them."

A Taste of Paradise

Rav Avraham Haim, one of the pupils of Rav Moishe Leib Sasover, wrote the following story about his teacher:

Once, when I was with my Rebbe, Levi Yitzhak of Berdichev came to visit Reb Moishele Leib Sasover late on a Friday afternoon.

"Moishe, I'd like to be with you for *Shabbes*."

"Then you'll have to come with me, because I'm going to the water carrier's to eat."

I thought to myself that if Rav Moishe Leib Sasover was to spend *Shabbes* with the water carrier, he must be one of "them," one of the *lamed-vav zaddikim*. So I asked if I might come.

"Sure. Why not?"

We went to the outskirts of the city. The water carrier had a wife and eight children and the whole family lived in a hole. Everything was crammed into one little room. I don't want to say anything bad, but the place smelled terrible.

Rav Moishe Leib brought a little wine with him and Reb Levi Yitzhak, two challahs for *Shabbes*. We prayed, made *kiddush* over the wine, a *motzi* over the bread. Then Rav Moishele Sasover said, "Do you have a little something to eat, *lekoved Shabbes*, in honor of *Shabbes*?"

The wife of the *lamed-vav zaddik* said to my rebbe: "I knew you were coming, Rav Moishele, so I saved some of my sauerkraut from Pesah."

Sauerkraut from Pesah! In the middle of the summer. It goes without saying there was no refrigerator!

Friends, you can't imagine. She barely opened the lid of the jar and I almost fainted from the smell. But I didn't say anything.

First she gave a little bit to Rav Levi Yitzhak, who started to yell: "*Gan Eden*! *Gan Eden*—Paradise!"

Then she gave a taste to Rav Moishele Sasover who, with the barest drop in his mouth, *mamash*, keeled over and began yelling: "*Gan Eden*! *Gan Eden*! This sauerkraut is straight from Paradise!"

Then she gave a little bit to me. I barely made it to the door before I began vomiting everything I'd eaten since my *bar mitzvah*.

Rav Moishele came outside and helped me to my feet. "Let's face it, Rav Haim. You're not on the level yet. I think it's time for you to go home."

Moishele the Water Carrier

What does it mean to be in exile? That I don't know anymore how to pray because, since the Temple was destroyed, I haven't been able to daven *properly. The moment a person prays on the level of Kingdom,* Malchut, *with all his strength, he is free. But if he cannot concentrate, then the "Other Side" has dominion over him. When I try to pray and can't, then I know I'm in exile.*

What does it mean to have a covenant with somebody? In the midst of all the darkness and stupidities that could bring one down, I can turn to that person completely. To have a covenant with God means I can be in the lowest depths, but in one second I can turn my heart to God and shake off the dark tyranny of the Other Side.

oishele the Water Carrier lived next door to Ivan the Magician. Now Ivan earned thousands. I don't mean he was an ordinary magician with smart tricks like you see on television. Ivan knew the real secrets of heaven and earth, powerful secrets from the "Other Side" and he was not adverse to using them for his own personal benefit.

One day, Moishele couldn't bear his own poverty anymore. He went to Ivan and said: "Magician, I want to become your follower."

Ivan pointed to the couch. "Sit down. I'll have to hypnotize you first."

Moishele lay down and Ivan said: "Okay, now. Forget your name."

Forgotten.

"Forget all the names you've ever so much as heard in the world."

Gone.

"Forget those you love, your wife and children."

Wiped out. Erased.

"Forget your father and mother."

Done.

"Forget there's only One God."

Moishele jumped out of his trance. "What! I can't do that!"

"Why not?"

"Because I'm a Jew!"

"So, forget you're a Jew!"

"How can I when there's only One God?"

The Ugly Woman

On the negative side, one of two things can happen to us when we come into the world—we may become dirty or we may become ugly. What, you might ask, is the difference between the two? Dirty means that, while I have made mistakes, I'm still myself. I can wash my face with my own tears. But if I'm ugly, I don't even have my own face anymore. This is something I cannot fix myself. I'll need someone else to cry for me, their tears.

here was once a bright young man who was in love with wisdom. He went from one house of study to the next to learn Torah from the best teachers of his time. He traveled on until, finally, he reached the *yeshivah* of the wisest rabbi in the world.

His teacher was indeed extraordinary but, the young man soon learned, he didn't know everything. The very first day, the young man saw that each time the great rabbi faltered over a question, a paper would fall from the women's gallery overhead. The *shammes* would fetch it and bring it to the rabbi, who would read it and only then offer the correct answer.

It was very clear to the young man that these little notes from above weren't rain. Perhaps they were *mannah*, heavenly wisdom, but he was quite sure someone was writing them. He asked the other students who this brilliant person could be. At first they were reluctant to answer but he persisted until one finally confessed:

"The rabbi's daughter is an amazing scholar, even wiser than her father. She sits in the women's gallery listening and learning. Whenever her father stumbles over a question, she writes the answer and throws it down to him."

Now the young man was not just seeking great knowledge. He was also looking for a wife. When he heard about the rabbi's daughter and her remarkable wisdom, he immediately inquired if she were married or engaged.

"Her? No."

The young man asked all the students: "Who is this woman who throws messages from above? Is she old? Is she young? Why didn't she get married yet?"

Everyone's response was the same. "She's the rabbi's daughter. All day she sits and learns. More I cannot tell you."

The young man thought about the rabbi's daughter day and night. He became, sight unseen, completely obsessed with her. "What an honor it would be to have such a wise woman for a wife," he thought to himself.

Again he went on inquiring about the girl. "At least tell me what she looks like!" he would say.

But they would not answer.

It didn't really matter because, by this time—

sight unseen–he had fallen completely in love with her. But he never could meet her. The young scholar became so tormented that he decided there was only one thing to do. He summoned his courage and went directly to the rabbi:

"Exalted rabbi, tell me, yes or no. May I marry your daughter? I've never seen her, but I know she's an exceptional scholar. I'm so impressed with her wisdom that I've already fallen in love with her."

Rather than rejecting the young man's offer, the rabbi seemed to take it seriously. He studied the young man's face, asked him many questions about himself and stroked his beard as he considered the matter very carefully. There was a profound silence in the room as the rabbi deliberated.

"Yes," he finally said. "It's possible for you to marry my daughter, but on one condition. You will not be allowed to see her until after the wedding."

Everybody knows that according to Jewish custom, a couple cannot get married unless they have seen each other at least once before the wedding. God forbid they should marry and not be attracted to each other. This would be a disaster.

The boy was overjoyed. As far as he was concerned, all obstacles to his marriage had been overcome. And so he answered immediately.

"Her appearance doesn't matter to me. I'll marry her anyway."

The great rabbi was very stern. "Please, don't

answer without thinking. Take a week, think it over. I want you to understand what it means not to be permitted to see your bride until after the wedding."

But what can you do? The student never really questioned his choice, certain this was God's will. He was so in love with her knowledge, he imagined his bride to have a body as exquisite as her mind. He was in a state of bliss. A week later, at the appointed time, he appeared before the rabbi to make his formal proposal.

"Great rabbi, with your permission, there's no question in my mind. I must marry your daughter."

The wedding was celebrated; the young man never saw his bride. Her face was heavily veiled. He knew only that she moved gracefully, that she was beautifully dressed. Judging from her outward appearance, he imagined her face to be supernally holy, like Eve's in the Garden of Eden.

After the wedding, the couple rode home together. They entered their house and sat on chairs facing each other, alone for the first time. When the young man with trembling hand reached to lift her veil, she stopped him.

"I know my father made you promise not to look at me until after the wedding. Now I too must ask a condition of you. Before I show you my face, promise me that, no matter what happens, you will remain with me this one night."

"This one night! How can you say such a thing? I will be with you forever!"

Her face still heavily veiled, the woman slowly shook her head. "Please—don't promise what you cannot give! You will leave me after this night. But if you will be a husband to me, perhaps God will bless me with a child."

The young man was bewildered by her strange talk, but gave his word.

When the rabbi's daughter lifted her veil, the young man screamed and screamed. The woman's face was absolutely frightening. Ugly is not the word. Her countenance was completely misshapen—part animal, part woman. She had the face of an ox, for when her mother had been pregnant with her, the woman had been attacked by a wild bull. The mother's fear of being gored by the beast had been so great that the baby took on the imprint of the image of the ox.

There are thousands of tales from those times of cases where a pregnant woman was frightened and her baby—God forbid—inherited the imprint of her fear. But this young woman was felt to suffer more than any because clearly, she had a beautiful soul.

Needless to say, the groom was in such a state of terror that he wanted nothing more than to turn and run. But he kept his promise to stay one night with his bride, in order to consummate the wedding.

The young woman, being full of understanding, felt his horror, his fear of being possessed, how difficult it was for him to be true to her. But, knowing this was the one time in her life she might know love, she received him and was thankful.

Before dawn, the groom slipped out of the bed. The bride lay still, pretending to sleep, listening as he hastily packed his belongings. The last thing the young man did was to leave his *tallit*, the prayer shawl she had given him as a wedding present, beside her veil on the chair. He ran out of the house and was never seen in her community again.

This was a tragedy but, *Baruch HaShem*, the craziest, most wonderful miracle happened. The rabbi's daughter had a little boy who was not only beautiful to behold, but wise, like his mother. He was happy but curious. Like all children he would constantly question his mother: "Where is my father? Why can't I see him?"

When the child was young, his mother would always answer: "I don't know, but here is his *tallit*. When you are *bar mitzvah*ed I will give it to you."

"Why isn't he living with us as other fathers do?"

"Please, you're too young to understand. When it's the right time, I'll explain everything."

On the day of his *bar mitzvah*, the boy turned to his mother. "Now that I am a man, I want you to tell me the truth." His mother told him the reason why his father had left on their wedding night. The young man was shocked. For thirteen years he had grown up admiring his mother. He had no fear of her. In fact, he thought his mother was so beautiful that he couldn't understand why his father wouldn't appreciate her.

And like all young men with a good heart, he thought he could fix the situation. "How could my father be so wrong? I've got to find him, talk to him and bring him back to you!"

"Please don't. You will only bring me to shame because he will never, never come home."

Once the young man began to think about his father, he became obsessed. He was sure that if he could find his father, he could reunite the family. He began to think of nothing but this search. His mother, realizing he was never going to relinquish this hope, finally gave him her blessing to go.

The boy went forth on highway and sea, looking in Jewish communities everywhere, until finally he reached Istanbul. Just as he entered the Jewish ghetto, a funeral procession passed, accompanied by a very large congregation. Judging this to have been an important member of the community, the young man asked a bystander: "Who died?"

"The wife of our rabbi passed away in the night."

The young man, by this time, had searched near and far without finding his father and was greatly in need of advice.

"Tell me about this rabbi. Is he holy? Could I

learn many secrets of Torah and Kabbalah from him? Could he advise me on personal matters?"

Everyone told him: "What a great man our rabbi is! An inspiration! He must certainly be one of the wisest men in the world. There is no question he cannot answer for you."

"After his week of mourning is complete, I must go to this rabbi and ask him to help me find my father," the young man said to himself.

The next *Shabbes*, the young man went to the synagogue of the great Rabbi of Istanbul. He wanted to pray close to him, but the Rabbi was always surrounded by his most devoted followers. So the boy covered himself in his *tallit* and prayed the silent prayer alone, at a corner of the *bimah*.

As the rabbi was carrying the Torah around the temple, he noticed the young man and sent his *shammes* to ask him: "Who are you? Where do you come from?"

The boy told his name and that of his birthplace.

When the rabbi heard this, he was visibly overcome. He came over to the boy himself, shook his hand and said: "Please come to my house for *kiddush*. I want to know more about you and your life."

The young man thought that the rabbi's interest in someone from his birthplace might be because of his grandfather, who was still remembered throughout the Mediterranean as a great sage. But after services, as the young man walked through the streets of the Jewish Quarter with the rabbi, the wise man suddenly turned to him and asked: "Tell me how you came to possess this *tallit*!"

"My father left it with my mother on their wedding night. . . ." He then went on to tell the whole story, forgetting nothing. As he spoke, the rabbi became increasingly agitated. The boy presumed it was because of his wife's recent death. But when the boy turned to the great rabbi and said: "I appeal to you! Help me find my father," the man broke down and wept.

"I am your father."

The boy was astonished. "You! But then, don't you see! If I came to Istanbul the day of your second wife's funeral, this is surely a sign from heaven that you should return to my mother. Please, you must come home with me."

"My son, don't ask of me that which I cannot give! Stay with me and I will love you and be a father to you, but I cannot be married to your mother anymore."

The boy stayed several weeks. He and his father had long talks. They began to know each other. His father admitted, with some embarrassment, how in love he had been with his first wife before their wedding night. But whenever the young man would urge him to come home, the rabbi would again display his fear.

So the young man waited, hoping that with time and loving him, his father would change his mind. Every day that he stayed in Istanbul, he became more concerned. He knew his mother would worry.

Again the boy begged his father: "I must go back. Mother has been anxiously awaiting my return. Please, come with me."

But his father again refused, suggesting instead that the young man stay and follow in his footsteps as the rabbi of the community.

The boy stayed for close to a year, waiting for his father to have a change of heart. Finally, the young man realized that his request would never be answered. His father would not give in. So, early one morning, he disappeared from his father's house and started home, by sea and highway, to his mother.

It took him a long time to reach the place where he had been born. As he hastened, the young man was guided by the image of how overjoyed his mother would be to see him again. But the closer he drew to his village, the heavier his heart became. How could he tell her the truth about his meeting with his father?

How would she feel knowing that her husband still did not want her? It would be just as she had warned: he would bring her to shame.

The young man was torn. He knew there could

be no concealing his father's choice. His mother would sense the truth the minute she saw her son.

"How can I return if it will cause her such suffering?" he cried out in one moment and then, in the next: "How can I stay away? I must not disappear as my father once did."

For the first time he understood what his mother had gone through in losing her husband, and it broke the young man's heart. He threw himself on the ground and wept. "Master of the Universe, how can you make my mother so full of understanding, yet deprive her of love?"

As he cried bitterly, an old peddlar suddenly appeared on the road. Shaking the boy, he asked him the cause of his grief. Though the man was a complete stranger, the boy desperately recounted the whole story to the peddlar and asked what he should do.

The peddlar answered immediately: "You must go home! She's been waiting for news of you!"

"But what will I tell her?"

"First, before telling her anything, you must give her a present. I have the perfect gift." Rummaging in his pack, the old peddlar handed him a bottle of the sweetest-smelling perfume.

"Tell her to pat it on her cheeks and rub it across her face. It will make her feel very good. And here, take this mirror with you as well."

Before the young man could recover enough from his surprise to pay the peddlar, he was gone.

The young man continued on his journey home. When he finally arrived, mother and son embraced, happy to be together again. Before she could ask him any questions about his search, the boy gave her the bottle of perfume and repeated the peddlar's instructions on how to apply it.

Laughingly, the mother splashed the perfume on her cheeks, all over her face. When she took her hands away, he gasped. Her countenance had completely changed. She looked now as she would have, had the ox never frightened her mother.

And he held up the mirror for her, as his mother was now beautiful, shining with splendor, her image as Heaven always knew her. For she had the face of her own soul, cleansed by her son's heart-broken tears.

And the son brought his mother, by highway and sea, to Istanbul to meet his father. Her husband received her with great joy. Here, at last, was the bride he had imagined in those youthful weeks when he had fallen in love with her wisdom and been so full of faith that he had married her sight unseen.

The Trisker Maggid

verybody knows that the Trisker Maggid never ate and never slept. Once, when Reb Baruch of Medzhibozh, the Baal Shem's grandson, met Reb Avromole, he asked the Maggid: "*Heilige* Reb Avrom, why is it that you never eat or sleep?"

"It's very simple. I didn't eat today because I was too tired from not sleeping all night. Last night I couldn't sleep because I was too hungry from the day before."

Rav Baruch got very angry. "Answer me or I'll tear you out of both worlds." And he could.

So the Trisker Maggid told him the truth:

"Everybody knows that my father, Reb Motele, wouldn't speak before praying in the morning. One morning, however, he woke me very early and said: 'Avrom, get the horses ready. We are going for a ride!'

"I was only nine years old and it was a great honor for me to go somewhere with my holy father. Besides, something very special was happening in the world that day. I can still remember riding through the forest alone with my father, how every leaf, every tree seemed to shine with light.

"Eventually we turned off the regular path and went along a rough trail through the underbrush until we came to an old broken down shack. My father stopped the horses, handed me the reins and said: 'Wait for me here.'

"He went into the hut and stayed for over an hour. When he came out, he was walking with a young man.

"Baruch, you remember how my father's face used to shine from one end of the world to the other? This man's face was blazing with light. The two men were talking. I couldn't hear what they had to say. Only when they came near to the cart, the young man turned to my father and asked: 'Are you sure this is what you have to tell me?'

"My father answered: 'Yes. This is what I must tell you.'

"Then they both began to weep. They embraced each other and cried and cried. When their lamenting subsided, they kissed each other farewell, as if they wouldn't see each other for a long time, and my father climbed onto the wagon. Without looking back, he lifted the reins and sent the horses at top speed through the forest.

"When we reached the road, we slowed down. The whole time my father was silent, stared straight ahead, deep in thought. I was too afraid to speak to him. Only when we came in sight of our house did I ask: 'Father, who was that man?'

"'Mashiach ben David,' he answered me. 'The Messiah.'

"'The Messiah! Here! Now! But what did he want from us?'

"'He asked me whether or not it was time for him to come. I had to tell him the terrible truth, that nobody is really waiting for him yet.'"

And so the Trisker Maggid said to Rav Baruch: "If you had seen the Messiah and knew he wasn't coming into the world yet because no one was really waiting for him, could you ever eat or sleep?"

When the Messiah Comes

When Mashiach *comes, there will be no warning.* Mashiach *will come when we least expect him.*

One summer's night when the Yehudi HaKadosh and the holy Psziszher were sitting and talking together, the Yid HaKadosh asked his pupil: "How do you envision the coming of *Mashiach*?"

The Psziszher thought. "It will be a night like this. People will come home, eat dinner and go to sleep. In the middle of the night, there will be a great tumult out on the street. Some will wake up and ask: 'What's happening?' People will open their windows and yell to those below: 'Hey! What's going on?'

"And someone will yell back: '*Mashiach* has come!'"

The Yid HaKadosh reflected for a while. Finally he said: "Yes, it will be a night like this. People will come home. They'll eat dinner and go to bed. But one thing I see will be quite different."

"What's that?"

"No one will be able to sleep."

My sweetest friends, these stories are to help keep us awake until that great day–may it come soon! LeHaim!

Glossary

aron hakodesh The ark in a synagogue where the Torah scrolls are kept.

azut d'kedusha Holy *hutzpah*; holy arrogance; the ability to do a rightful deed even though, on the surface, one is transcending prescribed rules of conduct.

baal teshuvah (pl. baalei teshuvah) One who repents or regrets being far from his faith and returns to Judaism.

bar mitzvah Initiation of a Jewish boy into manhood at the age of thirteen, at which time he assumes full responsibility for his actions and can join the *minyan*.

Baruch HaShem "Blessed Be the Name." An expression of thankfulness indicating that all fortune comes from God.

beis din A Jewish court presided over by three, twenty-three, or seventy-one judges.
beis midrash House of worship and study.
bimah The platform in a synagogue from which the rabbi or cantor calls the *minyan* to prayer.
challah Braided egg bread made especially for *Shabbes* and holiday meals.
cretchma An inn. *Cretchmir*, an innkeeper or bartender.
cullot Embroidered coat worn by certain *hasidim* for religious occasions.
daven To pray.
foigel Bird.
Gan Eden Garden of Eden.
Gemora The Talmud.
gevalt Term similar to "oi," which may be used either positively or negatively to suggest a powerful or overwhelming experience.
gurnisht Lit., nothing. Worthless.
hassan The bridegroom at a wedding.
hasid/hasidim From the word *hesed*, meaning "compassion"; this refers to followers of the holy Baal Shem Tov and the generations of rebbes and students who carried on and developed that tradition.
has veshalom Lit., "pity and peace." An expression of supplication, figuratively used to mean "God forbid."
Havdalah Final ceremony in the observance of *Shabbes*. Following the third meal, this ritual uses a braided candle, fragrant spices, wine, and a spe-

cific prayer to separate the holiness of *Shabbes* from the new week.

heilige "Holy," an address used to show great deference and respect to a rebbe or certain students of the rebbe.

hevrah Group of *hasidim* who rally around a teacher (rebbe), studying together and looking after each other's welfare and self-development.

hevrah kaddisha The group whose job it is to prepare bodies and to bury the dead.

hutzpah While meaning "arrogance," this term is often used with respect to indicate someone with the courage to take an important risk in order to accomplish a goal.

kaddish Prayer for the dead that requires the presence of a *minyan*.

kapote Long black coat traditionally worn by the *hasidim*.

kavvanah Intention of will, concentration of one's prayer toward the highest goal. Linked to the depth of one's devotion and one's focus on God.

kefitzat haderech A miraculous journey in which those who travel reach a far-distant goal in a matter of minutes or hours rather than many days or weeks.

kiddush Prayer over wine said at the first two meals of *Shabbes* and on all major feasts for holidays.

Kol Nidre Opening prayer for Yom Kippur.

kvittel Note written by a supplicant to ask the rebbe's intercession with Heaven.

lamed-vav zaddikim *Lamed-vav* is the number

thirty-six in Hebrew. The *lamed-vav zaddikim* are the thirty-six most righteous beings who hold up the world. Because of their great powers as holy men, they remain hidden. The holy Baal Shem Tov was considered the head of the *lamed-vav zaddikim* until he chose to reveal himself to the world.

lekoved Shabbat Lit., "In honor of *Shabbes.*" In order to distinguish *Shabbes* from the week, one does not work, wears special clothes, prepares a more elegant feast, and in every way treats *Shabbes* as an important guest.

Maariv Evening prayer.

Malchut Lit., "Kingdom."

mamash "Really"; something tangible or real.

mannah The heavenly nourishment that God gave to the Jews to sustain them during their struggle to survive in the wilderness.

maseh Tale.

mazal Luck; fortune.

meshugena Crazy person. *Meshugas*, craziness or crazy actions.

mikveh Rain water or any water untouched by human hands in which the religious man makes his daily ablutions, especially before the Sabbath or when he feels he needs purification.

minyan Quorum of ten men necessary to make prayer communal rather than individual.

mishkan The house where God dwells.

misnagid (pl. misnagdim) Opponents of Hasidism who emphasized scholarship and the study of the Law, whereas the universality of the early hasidic movement made it accessible even to the illiterate.

mitzvah Good deed or action, especially one of the 613 commandments in the Torah.

motzi The prayer over the breaking of bread that comes after *kiddush* and the washing of hands at the beginning of a feast. The blessing is said whenever bread is eaten.

nebach Absolute zero, a wipe-out. Figuratively used in cases where one might say, "Poor thing."

Neilah Final and highest prayer of the Yom Kippur ritual of atonement.

neshamah Soul, meaning the most universal aspect of one's soul.

oi, oy Expression of ultimate bewilderment and frustration.

parshah Portion of the Torah. The five books of the Torah are divided into portions that coincide with the religious calendar for the year. Each *Shabbes* is called by the portion that will be read in the synagogue that week.

pasquinach One whose behavior in every respect shows poor habits, poor character.

patsch Slap.

Ribona shel Olam Master of the Universe.

schlepper Helpless soul, good-for-nothing.

schnorer Beggar.

sechil Guts. The kind of wisdom or sense to know what action to take.

sefer Holy book.

Shalom Aleichem Lit., "Peace be unto us." A greeting.

shammes The caretaker/guardian of a synagogue.

Shechinah The Presence of God, which dwells in

the world and, wherever found, showers great blessings and holiness.

shicker A drunkard.

shul Synagogue.

simhah Joy, bliss.

streimel Fur hat worn by certain hasidic sects.

tallit Prayer shawl.

talmid hocham Talmud scholar.

tefillin Phylacteries, the leather straps and boxes bearing the written text of the *Shema*, placed on the forehead and wrapped round the arm in fulfillment of the *mitzvah*.

tehillim Psalms.

teshuvah Repentance, return.

torah A heavenly teaching, often oral.

Torah Scroll containing the Five Books of Moses, comprising the history of the Jews and the essential teachings of their law.

tzedakah Charity. Jews very often promise *tzedakah* when requesting special aid.

yenta One who never stops talking; a gossip or complainer.

yid, yidele (pl. yidden) A Jew.

yiddishkeit The body of Jewish teachings, including the Torah and Talmud and all commentaries, philosophy, and mysticism, as well as learnings related to ritual observance. Although Reb Shlomo says: "It is deeper than the teaching; deeper than the doing. It is the ALL of being a Jew and living like a Jew."

zaddik A completely righteous person.

zechut Merit.

zeide Grandfather.

About the Authors

Shlomo Carlebach was a descendant of a prominent European rabbinical family dating back to the fourteenth century in Germany. Rabbi Carlebach immigrated to the United States in 1939 with his family and was the Rabbi of Congregation Kehilath Jacob, the Carlebach Shul, in New York. Rabbi Carlebach is regarded as the father of Jewish music. His compositions, which are based on psalms and phrases in Jewish liturgy, have, since the 1950s, become synonymous with Jewish celebration and prayer. Appearing in concerts worldwide, his guitar playing, storytelling, wisdom, and melodies touched thousands. Although he chose to reach the world through his artistry and entertainment, his true contribution to the Jewish world remained as an erudite scholar and sage. Rabbi Carlebach died in 1995.

Since her conversion to Judaism, Susan Yael Mesinai, an artist and writer, has devoted her life to Jewish causes. A resident of New York City and Israel, she is best known as the founder and director of the ARK Project, which investigates the fate of Raoul Wallenberg and other prisoners of war.